Secrets in a House Divided

Clara Silverstein, in this historical (and yet entirely contemporary and all-too-relevant) novel, brings a world, a place, a human experience to full life with her wild insight, her hot-wired imagination, and her boundless empathy—tempered with realism, infused with clarity. Her prose is poetry, but this lyricism never hides its truths. In this work we find the real to be as terrifying as we suspected, and the spiritual to be as sublime as we never dared hope. This is the book we need right now, and the writer whose vision for whom we've been waiting. You will read *Secrets in a House Divided* without wanting to put it down, but you will return to it over and over again—looking for the beautiful sentences you highlighted, reliving the scenes that felt, as you read them, both feverish and hallucinatory, so visceral they might have been moments experienced in your own life. Nothing more can be asked from a writer, or from a reading experience.

—Laura Kasischke, National Book Critics Circle
Award Winner and author of nine novels,
including *The Life Before Her Eyes*

Like the best historical fiction, *Secrets in a House Divided,* set in Civil War Richmond, is replete with details of the day-to-day lives of those impacted by the war. The story of Amanda Carter, a young mother left on her own while her husband fights for the Confederacy, is a story of struggle and ultimate redemption. Like all of us, Amanda is flawed and complicated; she is equally fascinating and resilient. Her relationship with her extremely capable slave Cassie as they navigate one obstacle after another, is the central relationship of Amanda's life. As Amanda grows and learns to accept herself for who she is, we consider our own capacity for honesty and forgiveness. Part love story, part tragedy, part war story, *Secrets in a House Divided* is everything we want in a novel.

—Marjory Wentworth
South Carolina Poet Laureate

Against the tumultuous backdrop of Civil War Richmond, Clara Silverstein's lush and vivid novel takes us into the worlds of women across the color line, mistress and slave, whose lives are forever changed in a transforming time. The "secrets" in this "house divided" are the stories they share among themselves—and the lucky reader—yearnings and heartbreak for the men they love and lose, and the children, against all odds, they struggle to protect in a perilous world. Rich in period detail and wise in matters of the heart, this compelling tale captivates a reader with the immediacy of history and the high drama of the home front, while providing emotional uplift, too.

—Roy Hoffman, author of
Chicken Dreaming Corn
and *Come Landfall*

Secrets in a House Divided

A Novel of Civil War Richmond

Clara Silverstein

MERCER UNIVERSITY PRESS | *Macon, Georgia*
2018

MUP/ H963

© 2018 Clara Silverstein
Published by Mercer University Press
1501 Mercer University Drive
Macon, Georgia 31207
All rights reserved

9 8 7 6 5 4 3 2 1

Books published by Mercer University Press are printed
on acid-free paper that meets the requirements of the
American National Standard for Information Sciences—
Permanence of Paper for Printed Library Materials.

Printed and bound in the United States.

This book is set in Adobe Caslon.

ISBN   978-0-88146-669-0
ISBN   eBook   978-0-88146-670-6
Cataloging-in-Publication Data is available from the Library of Congress

For my mother, Ann, who taught me curiosity about Richmond history

Chapter One

Amanda cannot see what has snagged inside her. It's no bigger than a marble, yet it weighs her down, draining her pride, her respectability, her will to stand up straight. She spends the days dizzy, one minute thinking that a walk in her garden will do her good, the next slumped on a bench with her handkerchief against her mouth.

The predicament of pregnancy torments her. At night, she wakes, the dark choking her like dust, ashamed of herself and fearful of every punishment that is to come. She's become pinch-mouthed and impatient with her four-year-old daughter, Nell, too often pushing the girl off her lap. Nell's eyes grow sodden and imploring with the constant rejection.

Amanda dares not speak of her troubles to anyone, as if closing her mouth will somehow close off her head from the rest of her body. As if one day, she will wake up and go about her business without dizziness and panic. Soon she will have to tell her lover, Jed, poisoning the easiness of their afternoons in the arbor. Soon her condition will become obvious to him, obvious to everyone.

The war against the United States drags on and on, dispiriting the Confederacy. Union troops have moved close to Richmond, their cannon shots concussive enough to jar the windows in her home. The bell tower in Capitol Square rings an alarm so often she barely hears it anymore.

The nourishing warmth of April 1864 has given way to the damp, suffocating heat of May. On many mornings, Amanda directs Cassie, the house slave, to weed the tomatoes and cucumbers. Amanda dons a sunbonnet and gloves, then comes out with scissors and a basket. Nell trails behind them, sometimes picking up weeds, sometimes strewing them to wither on the paths between rows. Amanda gratefully harvests whatever they can grow because of Richmond's food shortages. Hungry people roam the streets, lurking behind the First Market to pick through the refuse, hoping for a scrap. The most they might find these days is a moldy potato peel, nibbled by rats.

The privations make everyone drawn and haggard. Only the pluckiest ladies manage to put on a brave face, mostly because it's good manners to be pleasant. Amanda has heard talk of "starvation parties" at which nothing is served but water.

Amanda's husband, Edwin Carter, enlisted in the Confederate Army in the summer of 1861. He went off to fight a little more than two years after they married. Amanda couldn't help but resent his cavalier attitude about abandoning her and their daughter. It was difficult enough for Amanda, only sixteen years old at the time of her wedding, to move into the home where Edwin had once lived with his first wife, a woman who died in childbirth. Now, with a daughter to raise, Amanda still feels unprepared to manage the household without him.

Edwin came home for a Christmas furlough in 1863, but Amanda hasn't seen him since. He writes her frequently, always beginning, "My Dear Wife." In his letters, he sounds more attentive than he did when he lived there with her in Richmond, preoccupied with secession and enlistment. His most recent letter arrived at the end of March and told of wind cutting through a crude winter hut in Orange County. "I look forward to the spring campaigns, if nothing more than to go on the march instead of waiting and shivering," he wrote. She has received no word from him for nearly two months. If he's still alive, Amanda imagines him gaunt, a shell of the proud man he was. Worse, he could be lying at the side of a battlefield, his broad chest torn open, bleeding to death, while his men fight on instead of tending to him. It does no good to worry about him. Her once-simmering anxiety has cooled to an ache that she surmounts by distracting herself in the garden—and lately, with Jed.

Amanda and Edwin Carter's home on East Grace Street sits high on a bluff over Shockoe Valley. In the late afternoon sun, the James River glimmers beyond the flat roofs of the hulking brick warehouses near the Richmond Dock. A ways upriver, the Tredegar Iron Works clangs day and night, the black smoke from its chimneys keeping pace with the Confederate cannons it forges. In the evening, when the constant clatter of wagons up Church Hill to the main hospital for wounded soldiers finally slows, Amanda can sometimes hear water gushing down the rocks. These falls kept the first party of English explorers from continuing up the James past Richmond. She wishes she could be a leaf in the current, spinning, going under and resurfacing, all the time moving swiftly, unimpeded, toward the coast.

Instead, she picks up the bandage that she is sewing from rags and asks Nell for the pincushion. All the hospitals in Richmond are in desperate need of bandages, and it's up to the ladies to make them. Nell picks up the cushion, pulls out a pin and pokes it back in, ignoring her mother's request. Tucked behind her ears, the ends of her raven-black hair are beginning to curl and snarl just like Amanda's. Her eyes are also like her mother's, the same bluebell color. Yet the contour of her round face and prominent jaw already look like a miniature of Edwin's.

"Don't be disobedient," says Amanda.

Nell holds up the pin and twists it so it catches the light from the parlor's front window.

When Amanda reaches over to take the pincushion, Nell drops the pin onto the rug.

"Now, look what you've done!" Amanda scolds.

Nell slides off the sofa, steps on the pin and wails.

Amanda sighs and sets aside the bandage. "Let me see your foot."

"Cassie!" Nell calls, running out of the room. "Help me!"

3

CHAPTER TWO

A few days later, Amanda hears the front door open and shut, then Cassie's quick, light footsteps. Only about five feet tall, Cassie moves with surprising grace for someone with wrinkles at the edges of her eyes and a bit of gray threading her hair.

"Any mail?" Amanda asks.

Cassie shakes her head and goes into the kitchen.

"Why doesn't my Daddy write me?" Nell wonders, fidgeting with the hem of her dress.

"He lives in a tent far away from here," Amanda tells her.

"What's a tent?"

"It's like a house, but the walls are made of cloth, kind of like a bedsheet."

"Oh," says Nell, turning away. "Where's Cassie?"

"In the kitchen. Go tell her it's time to do some gardening."

Amanda picks up the *Richmond Daily Dispatch* newspaper. Even though it's only mid-morning, her face and underarms are damp. Earlier, she twisted her hair into a bun, but tendrils are already escaping. Holding up the one-page broadsheet of newsprint, she scans the list of more than twenty-five killed, wounded, and captured men. Edwin would be listed as Edwin Carter, tobacco merchant, of Richmond. She thinks maybe he would be better off on this list than to learn of her unfaithfulness. Then she berates herself for such grim thoughts. Not seeing his name, she moves on to the "War News" article in the top left column of the front page. All seems quiet at Petersburg, the front about thirty miles south of Richmond, after the military repulsed three assaults the day before. A detachment sent to skirmish with the enemy near Cold Harbor found the lines of Union soldiers mostly deserted. It seemed that Union General Ulysses S. Grant had changed positions.

Amanda plans to pick a few beans today, then bring a basketful to the makeshift hospital that her neighbor, Mrs. Caroline Walker, runs in her home. Many of the men injured at The Wilderness and Cold Harbor have moved out, but her downstairs is refilling with soldiers from the front at Petersburg. It's a wayside hospital, designed for men due for an honorable discharge, convalescing until they are well enough to travel. The official hospitals have little capacity for anyone but the most gravely wounded and ill.

Amanda stands up, smoothing her everyday calico dress. The waist is tight, but the full skirt hides what's inside her. She feels unsteady, even more clumsy than usual with her nearly six feet of height and long feet. If Edwin comes home soon, everyone will assume the child belongs to him. Yet why would he possibly come home? Nobody seems to be able to get back to Richmond on furlough these days. She knows from the patients at Mrs. Walker's that soldiers who leave the war are either cowardly deserters or too wounded to keep up with the constant marches and skirmishes.

She swallows her queasiness, pulls a pair of work gloves from a basket by the back door, and steps outside. A blast of damp heat assaults her cheeks. She dabs the sweat off her brow with a handkerchief and keeps walking towards the cool air between bean vines. She can see a red cotton scarf tied on top of Cassie's head, and her brown arms darting between the green leaves.

Amanda forces herself to step into the first of eight rows of vegetables. The vines, tied to wooden stakes, climb up to her eyes. She relaxes as she concentrates, each pod warm in her fingers, the shape of a smile. Cassie hums as she works, her mournful melody weaving in and out of the buzz of bees.

When Amanda moves into the next row and crushes a tomato leaf, its peppery scent rises, along with her stomach. Just in time, she leans away from the basket. She shudders and wipes the edges of her mouth with her handkerchief.

In two strides in her bare feet, Cassie comes to her side. She assesses Amanda carefully through slightly narrowed eyes.

"Miss Nell, go and get your mama some water," says Cassie.

Nell ambles to the cistern, kicking a stick with her bare toe as she goes.

"Breakfast didn't agree with me," says Amanda.

"Soda biscuits generally agree with everyone."

"Not me. Not today." Amanda tries to smile but her mouth just twitches. "I'm fine."

Her face and neck feel clammy. The pregnancy with Nell wasn't nearly this bad, the fleeting moments of nausea barely interrupting her. Her condition felt like a sweet secret at first. When she told Edwin, he tenderly stroked her belly, tears in his eyes. It felt like a blessing four months into their marriage. After that, she blithely accepted Edwin's solicitousness and Cassie's ministrations as her due.

Now Cassie folds her arms across her chest. The crease between her eyes deepens. "Ought to sit down."

"Go on back to work," says Amanda. Then her stomach convulses again.

When Amanda can talk, she straightens her back. Sweat trails down her temples and she has knocked her bonnet askew.

Cassie continues to wait, the bees circling and swooping into the vines behind her. Amanda looks away as her tears spill, staining the front of her dress. If she tells Cassie, she will have to name what she did wrong. Right now, silence feels safer than the embarrassment of confessing to a slave woman.

CHAPTER THREE

Cassie blinks when she steps back inside the dim and sweltering kitchen. After quickly assessing the pantry, she moves to the stove, then wipes her face on her apron. While Nell and Amanda wash up, she pinches the ends off the green snap beans and places the beans in a pot. Dipping water from the kitchen bucket, she adds enough to cover the beans and sets the pot on the stove. She also fills and heats the teakettle. Then she goes back out to the garden, returning with a handful of peppermint.

There aren't many tools for fancying up food in this kitchen. She wishes she could reach for a fine mesh strainer from the long shelf at the Scruggs plantation, a place she left ten years before. Edwin's first wife, Mildred, lived there too, and Cassie worked for her and her family. Back then, Old Jenny started each day mixing batter for corn cakes and pulling out a griddle. As soon as the cakes were done, Cassie brought them out to Master and Missus Scruggs and their children. Cassie learned how to fold the napkins and lay out the silver just the way the Missus liked. While the family ate, she stood by the kitchen door, ready to clear dishes or fetch more food. In hot weather, she fanned the family until her arms grew sore.

Cassie's mama, whom everyone called Aunt Julia, worked in the house, too, looking after the Scruggs children and sewing all their clothes. Cassie's father worked on another place, Mama said, and there was no use talking about him because his master wouldn't let him visit no more. If the Scruggs children were napping and it was not yet time to set the table, Mama pulled out scraps of cloth and handed Cassie a needle and thread. When Cassie could sew a straight line, she began to hem and mend the the family's clothes.

As skilled as Mama was with fabric, she could not save herself the day she tripped while carrying a candle in the hall near Miss Mildred's room. Cassie heard the screams from the dining room and ran upstairs in time to see her mother helplessly waving her arms as flames circled her dress, then rushed up and turned her hair into a torch. Mama fell to the floor and writhed. Old Jenny rushed in with a bucket of water, then knelt by Mama and prayed. By then, all Mama could do was moan and reach for Cassie's hand. The butler grimly brought a blanket for Old Jenny to cover Mama's naked and charred body. The last Cassie saw, the butler was gently carrying Mama out of the room. Mama's blackened feet trailed from the blanket, toes pointing down. She never stood again. The next day, Mama was buried in the slave plot under the trees near the back of the cow pasture.

After that, Cassie began to take care of Miss Mildred. She set up a pallet in the corner of the girl's room. She missed her mother's warm bulk in the bed, but Miss Mildred's coughs and snuffles somehow soothed her. Cassie busied her hands with brushing the girl's hair, setting out her clothes each day, sewing for the whole family, and planting and picking vegetables with the gardener. All of the activity left her mind numb. Only when she began keeping company with Clancy, the stable hand, did she let another person see her tears. She named their firstborn Julia after her mother. Two years later, she gave birth to a son, Gabriel.

Old Jenny taught Cassie to brew peppermint leaves into tea for an upset stomach, straining them with a sieve. Tea is what Missus Carter needs now, but it won't help her for long. How foolish of Missus to think those trees in the garden could keep her and that lame soldier hidden. Cassie has always known what was going on back there. The low murmuring and flattened dirt beneath the bench, and their misarranged clothing, told her everything.

As Cassie sets the table for Missus Carter, she wonders whether to make clear that she knows what's wrong with her.

For a young, white lady, she has a sweet disposition, but she barely knows how to do anything except tend the garden. When Missus first moved to Richmond as Master Carter's new bride, she had no idea how to take charge of her own home. Cassie had to remind Missus to say what she wanted for dinner and then to write Cassie a pass for permission to go to the market and buy the provisions. When Missus became pregnant soon after she moved in, Master wanted her to rest so she wouldn't lose the baby like Mildred had. Once Miss Nell was born, Cassie had to take over Nell's care because Missus didn't seem to know how to do that, either.

Cassie worries about what Master Carter will do if he comes home and finds out about the secret child. He's a quiet sort, not given to carrying on with a loud voice and an upraised hand. Yet he might tell Missus to leave and slam the door behind her. Then he might want to sell his house and Cassie, too.

Cassie goes to the sideboard and picks up a small bell to summon the Carters for lunch. When they are seated, Cassie brings their plates from the kitchen. She sets a cup of the mint tea in front of Missus. "This will help," she says. But Missus takes one sip, then stands and rushes from the room.

"Mama!" calls Nell, getting up.

"Sit, child," says Cassie. "Your mama ain't feeling well."

Nell pats the chair next to her.

"Sit with me," she says.

"You know I can't do that here," says Cassie. "Dining room's not my place."

"But I want you to!"

Cassie picks up Nell's plate and carries it into the kitchen. The girl eats at the kitchen table while Cassie sits on her stool by the back door. Only when the white people finish can she eat her own lunch.

When Cassie hears the halting tread of Missus in the dining room, she goes to see about her. Missus looks at her with eyes the color of bleached indigo cloth. Cassie knows that Missus will listen carefully to whatever she has to say right now.

"I know a body that could help you."

Missus gasps. "How do you know what ails me?"

"Ways of mothers and babies ain't mysterious."

Missus blinks rapidly, as if her eyelashes might help her make up her mind, then lowers her head. "Tell me," she murmurs.

Chapter Four

The next day, Amanda woozily walks to the back of the garden and sits on a bench beneath a row of crape myrtle trees. The trees form a tunnel of shade with pink blossoms overhead and cool, green-tinged air underneath. At the back end of the tunnel, a brick wall rises, muting the rhythmic click of hooves against cobblestones and other noises from the street. The interior feels protected from the outside world as well as the house and the upper garden's vegetable rows. Maybe that's why she began an intimacy of the improper kind here on this very bench.

A bullet had shattered Jed's left foot by the time Amanda met him at Mrs. Walker's. At first, he was in too much pain to speak. His eyes, the same ruddy brown as the James River, followed her as she moved around the room with water and a kind word to help distract the men who didn't feel well enough to sit up. His hair and beard matched his eyes. When she bent to hand him a glass, he grasped her wrist lightly, his fingers surprisingly nimble, and thanked her. After he let go, she had to rearrange her hairpins to compose herself.

Several days passed, and then Jed was able to make his way out to the chairs under the dogwood tree and smoke with the other men. One afternoon, when Amanda brought a basket of the first strawberries from her garden, Jed asked her for a pencil and a sheet of paper.

"Do you need help with a letter to your wife?" she asked. She was used to taking dictation from men who had never learned how to write.

He shook his head. She continued offering strawberries to each man. Later, when she returned for her empty basket, he handed her a sketch of herself. In just a few quick strokes with the pencil, he made her look prettier than she felt. She wanted delicate features, and instead, she had blue eyes widely set beneath dark brows, and full lips under her broad cheeks. In the sketch, he managed to balance her features under the curls straying from her bun and give her a lighthearted smile.

"Why, you must be feeling better. Thank you," she said, her cheeks surely red enough for him to notice. She turned the sketch over, put it at the bottom of her basket, then later set it on the bureau in her room. Every morning, she sized it up, trying to compare her broad-faced, gawky vision of herself with what Jed saw.

When Jed first tried to move around on crutches fashioned by Mrs. Walker's gardener, Amanda realized that he stood just a little shorter than her. His freckles flashed like sparks on his pale hands. Doggedly, he propelled himself around the boxwood borders in the Walker garden.

"You're getting stronger," she encouraged him one day when he returned and practically collapsed into a chair. The crutches clattered to the ground in front of him. He pulled out a handkerchief and wiped his brow, then smiled at her.

"It's a mite harder going around this garden on crutches than marching with a haversack."

"Still, you get around."

"Next thing you know, I'll be dancing with you."

Amanda smiled as she imagined the one-two-three beat of a waltz with Jed's shoulder near her cheek and his hand at the small of her back.

"What did you think about when you were on the march?" she asked.

"Home, mostly. Prettiest place you ever saw, East Carolina. Pamlico River runs right through town and the sun turns all orange over the water every evening. When I was coming up, there was a passel of us kids down near the docks every day begging the sailors for a taste of molasses that came all the way from the West Indies."

"I've never left Virginia," she said with a sigh.

"Well, you're missing a sight."

"I'd like to see that part of the country on a pleasure trip one day."

"I wish I could show you personally, but a walking tour is out of the question right now," he said, smiling again.

Amanda tucked a strand of hair behind her ear. When Jed flirted with her, she did feel pretty. His banter relieved her resentment at being stranded by her absent husband. She chuckled, then left to refill a pitcher of water, embarrassing herself as she stumbled on a rock.

When Amanda returned, Jed handed her a sketch of the brick warehouses, docks, and wide, flat water of his hometown. She imagined herself walking hand in hand with him, his foot magically healed and both of them free to court each other, but she hastily admonished herself to stop thinking such balderdash.

"That's so nice, you should keep it for yourself when you feel homesick," she said.

When he folded the sketch to put in his pocket, an ambrotype the size of a postage stamp slid out and fell beneath the chair. He quickly leaned over, but couldn't maneuver himself to retrieve it. Amanda stooped and picked it up. A woman with puffy eyes, wispy lips, and flat hair on either side of a blade-straight part in the center of her scalp peered back at her. She looked angry. This must be his wife.

"I'll take that," he said, holding out his hand.

"What's her name?"

"Sarah."

"Do you have children?"

"Two sons. I'll take that now," he repeated, continuing to reach. "She don't belong in your hand."

Amanda placed the ambrotype in his palm and he closed his fingers around it.

As Jed's foot healed more and he traded his crutches for a

cane, Amanda began accompanying him on walks to rebuild his strength. His halting, lame gait made it easy for her to forget her own clumsy feet. There had been little courtship of this kind with Edwin. Their engagement was mostly a hasty arrangement. Jed's attention warmed Amanda after so many months of living alone in a bedroom filled with the dressing gown, hair oil, and other objects that Edwin left behind.

The day the tip of Jed's cane caught on a cobblestone and he faltered, she stepped close to him and held out her arm.

"Oh," he said with a grimace. "It hurts today."

"It takes time. You can't rush it."

Sweat dotted his forehead.

"Come in here and rest a little," she said, guiding him through her back gate and helping him to the bench. She went to the cistern at the side of the house and returned with a pail of water, a dipper, and a rag. After he drank and she wiped his face, she knelt to unpin the bandage on his wounded foot.

"Wait 'til we get back to Mrs. W—" he began, pronouncing the "w" more like a groan.

"You need help now."

As she worked the pin loose, he reached down and stroked the back of her neck. She boldly looked up. He ran his forefinger down her jaw.

Carefully, she placed the pin on the ground and rested her cheek against his thigh. The rough cloth scraped her skin. His hand smelled of the cigarettes he smoked. In the deep shade, she felt far from Cassie and Nell's faint voices trailing through the open windows of the house, far from Edwin's last letter. She stood up, dizzy, and sat on the bench beside Jed.

"Let me see where it hurts," she said, reaching once more for his foot.

He winced, then pulled her hand to his lips.

"It don't matter," he said, then wrapped both arms around her.

He kissed her, his tongue urgently circling hers, and the afternoon melted. When she stood to step out of her petticoats, they floated like foam around her ankles. She kicked them away and returned to the bench, where he lay on his back, his good foot on the ground.

Afterwards, she helped him walk around the magnolia tree and out the back gate. The tree's blossoms, intoxicating but edged with brown, had blurred to white blotches.

CHAPTER FIVE

The clang of bells makes Cassie smile. It's Sunday, the one day she can walk out the door without first seeing to Missus Carter and Miss Nell. She sits up, then kneels before the family shrine she has made near where she rests her head. For Gabriel, she arranged a ring of acorns and chestnuts because he collected both. On top of that, she placed a scrap of iridescent green cloth left over from one of Missus's dresses because Gabriel always liked anything green. For Julia, she sewed a rag doll that looked like the one Julia used to carry into bed with her. It wears a calico dress and a white bonnet, but Cassie left its face blank because she doesn't trust her hand to draw steadily on such a sacred thing. To remember Clancy, she keeps a scrap of a horse's leather halter that she found in the street in front of the Carter home one morning when she came out to sweep the front stairs.

In the gray light, she slips into the yard with her good dress over her arm. She fills a bucket from the cistern, then splashes water on her face and body, shivering a bit in the cool air. She dries off with a cloth, rubbing it against the wrinkled skin on her hands. Her shoulders haven't yet stooped forward like Old Jenny's, but she sees her stomach and breasts sagging. Her good dress, cotton in sage green, is remade from one of Miss Mildred's old frocks. Cassie took in the waist and added white ruffles to the front and sleeves. She wears it only on summer Sundays, so it's still in good condition.

Bowing her head, she murmurs, "Dear Lord, thank you for leading me to another day. Have mercy on my soul and on the souls of Clancy, Julia, and Gabriel. Keep me strong so I can one day see them again." She looks up at the magnolia canopy and silently thanks God for creating such green and glossy beauty on His earth.

The walk to First African Baptist Church takes Cassie

down the north side of Church Hill, where brick homes squeeze together more closely, eventually becoming row houses. It has been so hot and dry that her feet scuff up dust. She worries that her white bonnet and apron will be grimy when she arrives, so she slows down. When she hears footsteps behind her, she looks over her shoulder, then steps aside to let an elderly white gentleman in a top hat pass her. If she doesn't move out of the way fast enough, she risks a cuffing.

Cassie caught the spirit of the Lord back at the Scruggs place when she attended meetings led by a field hand who liked to preach. Old Jenny told her about the spot near the river where everyone met on Sunday mornings. Cassie, by then in her early teens, was used to being shunned by the folks in the cabins because she worked in the house. Yet at this gathering, smiles and nods welcomed her. She did nothing but listen for a few weeks, but then one day, when the preacher asked who would be saved, she fell to her hands and knees. The spirit came to her, lifting her body up above the red dirt, the silver whip of river, and the tobacco fields sprawled around her. He told her that she would find her mother when she went to glory, but the Lord would guide her footsteps until then. She must have fainted, because when she came to, Old Jenny and another woman were wiping her face with river water and saying, "Praise the Lord!"

Now, as Cassie passes the Virginia Central railroad depot, she looks up the tracks and wonders what it would be like to climb into a train car and ride away. The one field hand who ran away from the Scruggs place came back in chains and spent a month in what the slaves called "the shed," an old springhouse with a metal bolt on the outside. By the time he came out, he looked like a walking skeleton with scars looped from his chest to his back. He hobbled and spoke to no one.

The church, built into a sloping hill, looks wide as a barn. Its open shutters let the breeze whirl through before the crowd fills it up. Negroes from all over Richmond are allowed to gather here on Sunday mornings but at no other time. On the front walk, Cassie looks for her friend, Lizzie, a free woman who lives near the church and works with roots and herbs. When Cassie spots Lizzie's dozens of gray braids hanging below her bonnet like wisteria, she waves. The two women walk in together and take their seats at the end of a wooden pew.

A white preacher leads the services. He says all the right words, but he never gets worked up or brings any joy to the altar. His tepid entreaties about God ordaining obedience make Cassie close her eyes. Only when the congregation begins singing "Swing Low, Sweet Chariot" does she feel the spirit moving through her like warm water. In the horse-drawn chariot driven by the Lord, she sits next to Clancy, with one arm around Julia and the other securing Gabriel in her lap. They roll past green pastures speckled with violets and clover blossoms, up into the clouds. When the chariot stops, fog surrounds them, but she slips on the long white robe and golden slippers that an angel hands her, for once able to wear fine clothes proudly without facing the reprimand of acting too fancy and above herself. Arms around her children, she steps forward toward a light shimmering like the stirred-up surface of the river.

After the final prayer, Cassie descends back to a bench next to Lizzie instead of her family. As she walks out into the churchyard on bare, callused feet, she winces at the blaze of sun and heat. She turns to Lizzie and says, "Got someone who needs some help."

"What kind of help?" asks Lizzie, her plump cheeks shining with sweat.

"A baby she don't want."

Lizzie's eyebrows lift. "She white?"

Cassie nods. "And married. Got in trouble with a soldier."

"I heard that before."

"She lost her fool head. Might come to you, might not."

"I heard that before, too."

CHAPTER SIX

Carrying a basket of vegetables in the crook of each elbow, Amanda walks down the granite stairs in front of her house and out the gate. An ornamental cast-iron fence surrounds the front yard. The twisting pattern on the posts sets the fence apart from the others on their block of East Grace Street. Yet each red brick house on the street looks similar, with a porch not much wider than the front door held up by Greek columns. Each house also has two front windows on the first floor and three on the second floor. Because the Carter home is at the end of the block, its garden is larger than most, with high brick walls sheltering it from 26th Street.

Edwin chose the Church Hill neighborhood for its modern touches of gas lamps and cobblestone streets instead of dirt lanes. He also liked the sweeping view of Richmond's business district and the Thomas Jefferson-designed capitol perched on a hill in the middle of it. The house, Edwin believed, would make a statement to his older brother, who inherited the Carter family land in Amelia County, Virginia. Feeling cast out, Edwin found his way to Richmond and established himself as a tobacco merchant, selling what his brother and other plantation owners grew.

As Amanda walks around the corner on 26th Street and down one block to Mrs. Walker's home on East Franklin Street, she has to pay attention so her big feet don't catch on the uneven cobblestones. An ambulance wagon clatters by, jarring her. Since the fighting began circling Richmond in May, Amanda has gotten used to constant traffic headed to Chimborazo, the main Confederate hospital located a few blocks up the hill to the east of her house. That is where the most severely injured and ill men go. Those almost ready to return home are sent to Mrs. Walker's. Her husband, Reverend William Walker, spends most of his time at the Presbyterian church down the hill near the state capitol, leaving Mrs. Walker to oversee the makeshift hospital. In her finely tailored dresses, she leads Bible readings for the men each day from the lady's chair in her parlor. Lucy and Betsy, her house slaves, place sheets over the parlor sofa and the gentlemen's chair so the soldiers don't dirty the fabric. Pallets line the two back rooms. She and her husband reserve the rooms on the second floor for themselves. The slaves sleep above the carriage house.

Amanda wonders whether Richmond is really destined to fall, as some of the soldiers at Mrs. Walker's gloomily predict, or whether the tide of war will reverse. How long ago it seems that she and Edwin stood on Main Street as President Jefferson Davis arrived in May 1861 in Richmond, the new capital of the Confederacy. Citizens waved white handkerchiefs and shouted to welcome him as his cortege proceeded from the train depot to the Spotswood Hotel. Edwin barely hesitated to follow the call to serve his country, and left a few months later in September.

Mrs. Walker herself answers the door today, her spectacles shimmering. Above her lace-trimmed collar she wears a locket containing a photo of her husband. Her flint-colored hair sits obediently in its bun.

"Oh, Mrs. Carter, bless you. A new man is just getting settled today. It looks like you brought us something good to eat, too. Lucy will know what to do with this," she says, reaching for the baskets of beans.

Amanda steps inside. Despite sprigs of lavender in a vase on a table by the door, there's no way to disguise the smell of chamber pots and unwashed men.

"It seems to be quiet at the Petersburg front right now," says Amanda. "Maybe you will be less busy for a spell."

Mrs. Walker waves her hand dismissively. "We always have work to do. Betsy is just about to drown in that laundry kettle. Go help with the men in the back room while I read the others the Scriptures."

Amanda is accustomed to taking orders from Mrs. Walker. They met because Mrs. Walker recruited Amanda as a volunteer to help the Confederate cause soon after Edwin enlisted. She called on Amanda one afternoon, interrupting her as she weeded a row of carrots. Cassie answered the door and brought Amanda into the entrance hall. Mrs. Walker said, "I wanted to introduce myself to the new Mrs. Carter." Her upright posture and ribbon-trimmed sleeves revealed her gentility. Amanda felt disheveled, the front of her gardening dress dusty and unpresentable.

"Pleased to meet you," she forced herself to say, flinching at the reminder of Mildred Carter. Mildred's portrait still leaned against the wall at the back of the upstairs linen closet. Amanda had stumbled across it when she was unpacking her own linens. Crouching to get a better look, she saw a woman with a delicate, heart-shaped face and cheeks the color of dogwood blossoms peering back at her. Amanda's hands suddenly felt like they needed gloves for warmth. She stood quickly and spent the rest of the day in the garden, trying to crowd out the image of Mildred's dark, lustrous eyes.

Even though Edwin never talked about Mildred, Amanda always felt second best. Mildred Scruggs's family owned a tobacco farm in Dinwiddie County. She met Edwin in Richmond because her uncle was one of his clients. Amanda pictured a hummingbird of a woman in a forest-green moiré dress trimmed with lace, hovering about Edwin, quivering with nervous energy. She thought Mildred had probed the sweet center of Edwin, leaving Amanda the dregs.

Rushing right past Amanda's halfhearted greeting, Mrs. Walker had invited her to gatherings she hosted for neighborhood ladies to sew bandages for the Confederate cause.

"Helping the war effort will be a help to your husband while he's serving our country, and it will keep your spirits up," she said.

At the first meeting, Amanda quietly sat in a corner, embarrassed by her misshapen handiwork. Margaret, the aunt who raised Amanda after her parents died, used to nag her. "Bad stitches make bad britches." Amanda wanted desperately to sew straight, but the fabric always seemed to pucker when she tried to gently guide the needle.

"Come, join us," Mrs. Walker said to the new girl in the corner, holding a pile of fabric in her lap with one arm and gesturing with the other.

Amanda picked up her half-sewn bandage and scooted her chair closer. The half-dozen other women chatted about new enlistees whom Amanda didn't know. Still, she felt better hearing that other women shared her worries about the war and what would happen to the soldiers.

When Mrs. Walker announced to the sewing circle that she would start taking in wounded men, most of the ladies quickly found other less gruesome ways to help the cause, but Amanda kept returning. Even in their injured and weakened condition, the soldiers added variety to her trowel work and weeding with Nell underfoot, or waiting in the ever-growing lines at the market.

Today, after greeting Mrs. Walker, Amanda goes to the well and scans the garden for Jed. As she lifts the bucket, water sloshes out. "Clumsy girl," she mutters to herself. This is the second time today that she has splashed water on her shoes. Men cluster in the shade of the dogwood tree. A wooden fence and thick boxwood hedges screen the street. Those who can walk have moved the dining chairs outside. The ball-shaped feet of the chairs look misplaced in the dirt.

She spots Jed, his injured foot propped on an empty barrel, telling a joke. He blushes when Amanda comes outside, freckles temporarily disappearing under his reddened cheeks. Amanda admires the easy way he moves his hands, his delicate fingers tapping the air as he talks. He charms his audience.

"Not fit for ladies," he says, stopping in mid-sentence.

"Awww," says one of the men.

Betsy comes out with a tray of water glasses balanced on her reedy arms. With her colt-like gait and generous smile, she appears to be about twelve years old. Amanda thinks that soon enough, Betsy will learn the inscrutable demeanor of most slave women. Jed helps himself and then motions to Amanda.

"Good afternoon, Mrs. Carter," he says with a wink. She wonders if a flask has made the rounds while Mrs. Walker was reading Bible verses inside.

"Ready for your walk?" Amanda asks briskly. She leans over, inhaling traces of whiskey along with his usual sassafras scent. Men snicker. Jed grasps the chair arms and pushes himself upright, tottering. His bandaged foot thumps the ground. Amanda hands him his cane and he carefully takes one step. The men smoke.

"Steady now," says Amanda as she opens the gate to the alley. If they walk this back route, they are unlikely to encounter anyone who will observe them going into Amanda's garden. It might be more romantic to meet by moonlight, but it would be unseemly for her to call on him at a late hour. His efforts to propel himself with a cane alone in the dark would attract too much attention.

What she has to tell him will ruin their secret afternoons in the shade, their easy banter and urgent caresses. Each of her soft sighs during their lovemaking released just a bit of her anger at Edwin for his unremitting service to the Confederacy—and for his hasty choice of Amanda to replace the wife that he must have loved more. Jed's attention feels like sun breaking fog into ribbons of pale yellow silk. In their time apart, all she can think about is their next assignation, when they will cleave to each other like petals joining together to shape a bell.

When they arrive, golden but suffocating haze has suffused the afternoon air, making the crape myrtle shade welcome. As soon as they sit on the bench he takes her hand. His fingers feel sticky. She hears him breathing rapidly from the exertion of walking. Instead of moving close and resting her head on his shoulder, as she normally does, she swallows and removes her hand from his, clasping her fingers together.

"Jed," she begins, no more words coming out despite the careful speeches she has planned.

He removes his hat and places it in his lap.

"I sent word," he says, reaching for Amanda's hand again. This time she takes his hand and holds it between her palms. "They're expecting me home next week, as long as the rails don't get turned into Sherman's neckties and the trains still run."

"So soon?" Amanda asks. Her thoughts pinwheel. It was always so easy until now, losing herself in the whorls of hair on his chest, feeling her body spin. Everything has moved in circles this past month—their hands, their tongues, her hips. All the lambent parts of herself have surfaced in their hidden arbor. Now she feels exposed, like the branches over their heads have been chopped away.

"Say, now," he says, brushing her cheek with his free hand. "You knew it would come to this."

She nods, then blurts, "Don't you care what happens to me?"

"It don't matter. Your husband will come home."

"How do I know? I haven't heard from him. What happens to me?" she repeats.

He leans his head back and closes his eyes.

"There's more," she rushes on. "A baby!"

His eyes pop back open, roiled like stirred-up water. Amanda tries to meet his gaze, but he looks down. He pulls his hand free of hers and rubs his ankle.

"I reckon I should have known better," he says. "My foot the way it is, I thought I was all played out. I lost a lot of blood when I was wounded."

Amanda's heart thuds like a drummer leading a march.

After a pause, he says, "When was he last home?"

"My husband? Christmas 1863," she says. "Too long ago to be the father, if that's what you're thinking."

Jed's long fingers tap the bench.

Amanda crosses her arms and imagines running off with Jed, pretending Nell has been their daughter all along. Farming would be out of the question because of his damaged foot, but he could repair wagon wheels and tools. She could plant a garden and sell the preserves at the market. But what would become of Edwin, assuming he survives the war? Taking away his only child would be too cruel. Would Jed really stay with her, anyway? He might charm someone new, or go back to his wife.

"What are you going to do?" he finally asks.

"What can I do?"

He shakes his head. "Let me think on it. Maybe I can do something."

"What could you possibly do? You have a wife and children of your own."

"Oh, Amanda, my darling," he says, pulling her close.

At first, she resists his hand against her breast.

"Nothing else can go wrong," he says, and she gives in, unbuttoning her bodice, letting her hips glide above his body stretched out on the bench in the murky light.

CHAPTER SEVEN

The morning after speaking with Jed, Amanda wakes with a pounding heart. Rain taps the shutters. Gray light filters through the slats. She pulls strands of loose hair away from her face like clearing away fallen twigs after a windstorm. If Edwin were next to her, she could simply close her eyes again and pretend she carried his baby. Yet in her dream, he walked toward her, arms outstretched, face shriveled as a pumpkin left in the field in December. A rotten odor emanated from under his cap and his jacket flapped around his shoulders.

"I'm here," Amanda called in the dream, but Edwin kept walking. She continued calling and reaching out to him, but he never noticed.

This was not the Edwin she knew, whose confidence gave him a measured, stately gait. He had grown up on a tobacco plantation near the home of Amanda's aunt and uncle, and his brother still lived there. The day Edwin rode up on a sorrel horse to borrow a wagon from Uncle Chester, Amanda was coming from the garden with an armful of tulips that she had cut for Aunt Margaret's table. She wore a work dress with a tattered hem, and stray curls tumbled across her cheeks. After her uncle introduced them, she looked down into the purple bouquet of blossoms, too embarrassed to meet the eyes of the stocky man in polished riding boots. She had turned sixteen earlier that year and spent most of her time in the gardens with Nate, the elderly slave who taught her the ways of plants.

When Edwin asked where she cut the flowers, she raised her head again. He had an easy way with his horse, standing close to the animal's shoulder as he held the reins, clearly used to taking charge. Waiting for her answer, he stood without fidgeting, assessing her with kind eyes that were light brown with a hint of yellow. He was clean-shaven, with chestnut-colored bangs peeking out from beneath his hat. An aroma of pipe tobacco and horse leather wafted from him. His attention jolted her stomach and she felt warmth rushing to her cheeks.

"They grow in the garden down yonder," she managed to say.

"Could you see to my horse if I walk with this young lady a spell?" he asked Uncle Chester, who nodded with a wide smile that made Amanda suspicious.

As Edwin walked next to her along the path from the stable, a warm breeze stirred the young tobacco plants down the slope. He stood eye level to her, so Amanda wasn't embarrassed by her height as she led the way along the slate paving stones between the camellias and rosebushes. She wondered whether she sounded silly, but he nodded genially as she talked about each type of plant.

Edwin pulled Uncle Chester aside that day and asked permission to court her. Amanda felt flattered but also rushed. He planned to return to Richmond after inspecting his brother's spring tobacco planting, and he hoped to secure her hand before then.

"What good fortune that a gentleman has taken an interest in you," said Aunt Margaret. She always told Amanda to act like a lady because, with her awkward height and unruly hair, she would never find a gentleman on her looks alone. Now that the first suitor had unexpectedly arrived, Amanda felt overwhelmed.

"But he was already married once. And he's nearly twice my age."

"All the better for you. He has some experience in these matters."

"I might not suit him as well as his first wife."

"Nonsense! It's high time for you to marry. We can't keep you here forever, you know," huffed Aunt Margaret.

Amanda tried to picture herself married to the man she just met. Both of Amanda's parents had died when she was seven years old, and her aunt and uncle took her in. Amanda always felt like a misfit in the prim home. Maybe her own mother would have jollied her along when she pricked her finger with a needle or upset her sewing basket on the floor, but Aunt Margaret simply sighed in exasperation. When Amanda was twelve, she had embroidered a handkerchief with the initial "M" as a birthday gift for Aunt Margaret. After she presented it, Aunt Margaret squinted and rubbed the uneven stitches with her forefinger.

"Thank you. Your needlework is coming along," she said. Then she folded the handkerchief, put it aside, and never used it.

Amanda didn't feel much more welcome when she went to the village around Amelia County Courthouse. Marriage seemed natural for the young ladies who smoothly glided along in their full skirts, giggled coquettishly behind their hands, and ignored Amanda because they had not met her at the balls or socials for young people that they attended. Edwin, the sturdy man who had visited, offered what felt like her only chance, yet he wanted to take her far from all that she knew. He seemed kind, but would he suit her? She had not yet drawn close enough to him to determine how his cheek might feel against her face, nor whether his breath would smell of sage or crushed wheat. What he offered was a promise that she hoped he would keep.

The day after a simple wedding in her aunt and uncle's parlor in April 1859, a hired carriage brought the couple to Richmond. As they sat side by side on the wooden seat, Edwin put his arm around Amanda. The sensation of being touched with affection startled her. Her aunt and uncle never hugged her. On their wedding night, Edwin's hands had felt heavy as flat irons as he pushed up her nightgown and pressed against her. His urgency and grunts reminded her more of horses in the pasture than the blossomy feeling of gently swaying together that she had imagined. When he finished, the hair on his chest pricked her cheek.

Amanda watched the rolling tobacco and corn fields give way to thick stands of oak and loblolly pine. Edwin dozed while she peeked out at sun-dappled swaths of pine and maple woods. Pollens suffused the morning, giving the air a light chartreuse glow. Amanda thought it was a hopeful color to accompany the horses that clopped in steady rhythm. She was leaving her life as the orphan girl, ward of Aunt Margaret and Uncle Chester. In her absence, they would return to their orderly, formal meals with vases of cut flowers on the table, without the intrusion of a misbegotten young woman.

As the wife of a wealthy and respectable merchant, Amanda pictured herself becoming instantly glamorous and confident. She had read about Richmond, the state capital about forty miles east of Amelia County, in newspapers delivered a few days after they were published. In the sophisticated city, she could custom-order silk dresses to show off to her equally glamorous neighbors. Her shyness would evaporate and she would know what to say to everyone instead of feeling every word clump in her throat like a potato. No one would know that her mother had come from England to work as a governess and that Amanda's father had "taken advantage of her," as Aunt Margaret put it, and had to marry her to avoid a scandal. No one would again tell Amanda she was too interested in the garden instead of learning to be a sociable young lady. She wanted to unpack her first embroidered face towel and truly become Mrs. Edwin Carter instead of the awkward Miss Amanda Ayers.

When they reached the Mayo Bridge leading north into Richmond, Amanda sat forward for her first view of the city that would be her new home. The reddish-brown James River roared and splashed against the stone piers anchoring the bridge. A grid of buildings rose up the hill on the opposite bank of the river. At the top stood the white state capitol building fronted by tall columns to emulate a Greek temple. Several church spires and chimneys poked into haze that hovered above the scrim of trees.

After they crossed the bridge into the maze of narrow streets jammed with pedestrians and carts, Amanda wondered how the carriage driver would know where to go. She felt disoriented without the rolling fields and windswept, unobstructed views of the sky.

When the horse stopped on East Grace Street, Amanda peered out. Before her stood a brick house at the end of a row. A magnolia spread its limbs over the roof, making welcome pools of deep shade. Edwin opened his eyes and smiled.

Cassie came out to greet them, her feet bare on the clean-swept front porch, her brown dress cinched with a rope belt. She nodded but didn't smile, moving quickly down the porch stairs, her compact body strong but light. Beneath a red head scarf, Cassie's shrewd eyes assessed Amanda's rumpled dress. Amanda couldn't tell if Cassie would be sullen or obedient. Though she had spent many days with Nate as he tended the flower and vegetable beds, Amanda had little to say to the addled granny who was supposed to look after her or to the other Ayers house slaves, as her aunt and uncle always took charge of them.

The driver helped Edwin step down from the carriage. Though road dust smudged his coat and hat brim, he stood up straight, his shoulders wide enough to block the lowering afternoon sun. Pride swelled his smile wider than usual. He helped Amanda down and continued to hold her hand as she steadied herself on her cramped legs. "Welcome, Mrs. Carter. What do you think of your new home?"

"Well, it's—" Amanda began, overwhelmed by the houses set so close together along a cobblestoned street and the smell of manure left by passing horses. She was used to looking out her window and seeing a meadow where horses grazed, a row of barns for storing and curing tobacco, and a field beyond that filled with bobbing, sun-burnished wheat. The front yard here was so flat and narrow that a single row of rosebushes would fill it up. She wanted to say "peculiar," but instead she settled on "fine" so she wouldn't hurt his feelings.

Edwin tightened his grip and steered her through the iron gate. She took two steps, then climbed five bare, granite stairs. Fear roiled in her stomach. She knew she had to somehow walk in and make this place her own. The door opened into a hall with a polished wood floor furnished with a table and an umbrella stand. Stairs led up to the second floor. To the right was the parlor, where Edwin led her next. He helped her settle on the sofa, then went into the alcove next to it and picked up his pipe from the top of his desk. Cassie brought her a glass of cool water recently drawn from the well out back, efficiently setting down the glass and then darting right back into the kitchen.

When she had properly refreshed herself, Edwin led her through the dining room and kitchen. The back door opened from the kitchen to a wooden porch about ten by fifteen feet, with stairs that led to the garden. The afternoon sun slanted across the brick walls surrounding it. A few rosebushes budded along the path to the privy, but he pointed to the bare patches of red dirt dotted with acorns and magnolia pods.

"I see flowers here. All kinds of flowers that you plant. I know you have a hand with gardening, and this is yours. Before long, I hope we'll have little ones to help you out."

"Thank you," she said, blinking back tears.

"Now, now," he said, gathering her into his arms. His dusty coat chafed her neck. Though he was now her husband, he still felt like a stranger.

She wanted to glide through the grounds like Aunt Margaret, imperious and confident, but she felt unmoored. At the time, she hadn't realized how generous it was that he understood that the garden, a minor part of her aunt and uncle's acres, would surround her with something familiar and comforting.

Now, disoriented after her dream, Amanda sits up and pushes back the sheet with a sour twist of her mouth. Familiar objects in the room blur. The handle on the pitcher looks like an accusing hand on a lady's hip.

Cassie knocks lightly, then enters with a steaming cup of mint tea. Nell follows, holding her doll by the wrist.

After setting the tea on the bedside table, Cassie opens the wardrobe and asks Amanda what she would like to wear.

"This one, Mama," Nell says, tugging on a blue cotton dress with one band of white ruffles around the neck.

Amanda sighs. Even an everyday dress makes her feel like she's masquerading as respectable. She is about to answer that she plans to stay in bed all day when she notices the letter that Cassie brought in with the tea. Edwin has addressed the envelope in his unmistakably careful hand. He kept his ledgers from his tobacco warehouse so tidily that they looked like pages from a printed book. Though Edwin had no military training before the war, his calm competency and utter devotion to the Confederacy made him a successful soldier, eventually earning him his current position as a Lieutenant Colonel in an infantry brigade under General Jubal Early and Brigadier General John Marshall Jones.

"Take Nell back downstairs," Amanda orders Cassie. "Everything else can wait."

Nell pouts. "Mama, get dressed now."

Amanda waves her hand dismissively. After they leave, she rushes out of bed, barefoot and in her chemise, pressing her tongue to the roof of her mouth to still her nausea. She pulls back the curtain so she has enough light to read.

> *May 30, 1864*
> *My Dear Wife,*
> *You must be terribly uneasy about me after such a long interval of not receiving a word from me. I am putting pen to paper as soon as I am able. Right after I received your letter at our winter camp at Orange, the Spring campaigns began. The enemy crossed the Rapidan and we received orders*

to immediately march down the Orange Plank Road. At first, we drove the skirmishers away, but then the enemy struck back. I am sorry to say that General Jones, a brave man if ever there was one, was killed.

We continued on to Spotsylvania and built a salient that we nicknamed the Mule Shoe on account of its curved shape. We should have called it Broken Shoe for all the protection it offered to us. It was foggy and just at the break of day when the Yankees gained possession of the works and surrounded us. Most of the men left alive were taken prisoner. To my knowledge, they were sent to Morris Island, South Carolina. Owing to the fog, the enemy did not spot me right away, allowing me to escape to the rear, where I found the protection of a division that had been relieved of the trenches.

Right after this battle ended, I developed a bad headache. I then fell ill with a terrible fever, worse than anything I have ever known. I was out of my head for quite some time, not knowing night from day. When I began to feel better, I found myself in the home of a kind woman, Mrs. Clarke, still too feeble to lift my head or speak. There were other men in various stages of illness around me. She said I had typhoid and I was lucky to come through. Only now am I able to sit up with pillows behind me and pen these meager words to you.

What sustained me as I began to regain my senses was the thought of you, my darling, waiting at home for me with our dear Nell. I grow stronger every day and will soon again be in fighting shape. I am likely to be reassigned, given the losses that my regiment sustained, but I do not yet know where. Though I miss you more than words can say, it is my patriotic duty and my honor to continue serving our Confederacy. In the end, we will whip General Grant.

I send you my love and trust that the defenses of Richmond are strong enough to keep you and Nell safe until I can

once again be by your side.
      Please kiss Nell for me and take care of yourself.
      As ever,
      Edwin

Amanda holds the paper up to her nose. There is no trace of the rich tobacco scent from the pipe he smokes. He's still alive, yet he has already suffered much, and she knows how much more he will suffer once he learns of her deceit. She folds the letter and returns it to the envelope. How will she answer him? She needs time to think about that. As she opens her top right bureau drawer to put the letter away, she sees herself peering out from Jed's sketch.

CHAPTER EIGHT

In the dining room, Cassie brings Amanda her latest attempt at a coffee substitute: sprigs of thyme boiled in lightly salted water. Union blockades have prevented coffee and real black tea from coming to Richmond for many months. Cassie has tried brewing drinks with acorns, roasted corn, and chicory root. All of it tastes vile, as far as Amanda is concerned. She has taken to sipping plain water if sleep eludes her in the hours before dawn.

"Heavens!" says Amanda, setting her cup in the saucer with a loud clink. "This is the worst one yet!"

Cassie shrugs. What does Missus expect, fresh coffee beans with cream and sugar, too? "Well, Missus Carter, nothing much out there," she says.

Missus slips her napkin in and out of its monogrammed silver ring with fingernails she has bitten to the quick, fidgeting the way a child would. Her cheeks look pale as a peeled potato above her pouting mouth. Cassie wants to shake her shoulders and tell her that she needs to buck up and start facing the mess she made for herself.

Instead, Cassie goes back into the kitchen and returns with a wedge of cornbread topped with a spoonful of sorghum syrup.

"Try this," Cassie says.

Missus takes a bite, then holds her napkin in front of her mouth.

"Easy. Eat a little more."

"Why didn't Nell make me feel like this?"

"Every baby do different things."

"How do you know so much about it?" says Amanda.

"Two children of my own," Cassie blurts, then lowers her head and picks up her apron, squeezing the cloth in her hands. Her mother always warned her not to tell white people too much about her own business, because they might use it against her.

She silently chides herself for not showing more self-control. Yet Missus seems to think her troubles are the only troubles there are in this world.

Missus draws in a breath.

"I...I...I...oh," she manages at last. Then she plunges on. "What happened? Fever? Smallpox?"

Cassie hesitates, then decides she has little left to lose if she tells the whole story. "I got sold. Had to leave them and their daddy and come here with Miss Mildred when she got married to Master Carter."

"Didn't you...Couldn't you...?"

Cassie frowns. "Miss Mildred want me with her. Master Carter buy me. That's that."

Using her finger, Amanda dabs a drop from her saucer, then wipes it on her napkin. She finally says, "I'm sorry. You must miss them terribly."

Cassie turns away and walks back into the kitchen, her back hunched. She was expecting Missus to blink a few times and give her usual vague look. When Cassie comes back, Missus hasn't moved.

"Some hot water, Missus Carter?" she asks.

"Cassie? What are your children's names?"

Surprised, Cassie stops, the teapot in midair. Now she regrets divulging anything. The answer to that question feels too personal.

"Oh, never mind that," says Cassie.

But the Missus persists. "Do they still live with Mildred's people?"

Cassie forces herself to answer, her voice sloshing in the back of her throat. "Far as I know."

Missus draws up her forehead like a stitch pulled too tight. Then she signals for more hot water. Cassie pours and then hurries back into the kitchen before Missus has a chance to ask more questions.

CHAPTER NINE

Seated in the chair with a rose-carved back, Mrs. Walker reads from Romans 8. Her clear, ringing voice enunciates each word. *"For we are saved by hope: but hope that is seen is not hope; for what a man seeth, why doth he hope yet for? But if we hope for that we see not, then do we with patience wait for it."*

Amanda scans the faces of the men gathered around Mrs. Walker. When she doesn't see Jed, she slowly backs out of the room. She never feels stirred by such recitations. Her aunt and uncle made her go to a church filled with icy light, where she counted the number of floorboards while the preacher droned. Edwin stopped attending St. John's, the Episcopal church one block away from their home, after Mildred died. Only an unjust God would allow such a thing to happen, he told Amanda.

In the garden, Amanda once again looks for Jed.

"Some of the men left this morning, Mrs. Carter," says a man with pitted, weatherworn cheeks, looking up from a hand of poker. One of his elbows rests in a canvas sling.

Amanda feels her chest tighten, but tries to betray nothing. "I wish them all luck," she says.

"I'll be among them soon as I can travel," he says.

"Then I wish you luck, too," she says, turning to walk back inside.

In the corridor leading to the back room, she steadies herself by placing one hand against the wall. She knew this day was coming, but still, she thought she would see him one more time after telling him about the baby. Did he leave her a sketch or a note? She dares not ask Mrs. Walker.

Two new men have arrived since yesterday, occupying the closely packed pallets nearest to the door in the back room off the parlor. Beneath the window sits a trestle table, the only furniture remaining in the room. Bandages surround the ceramic basin on top. Amanda scoops water into a tin cup, then stands next to one of the new men, deciding whether to disturb him. He lies on his back, the crook of his left elbow shading his eyes, his right hand swathed in a bandage as thick as a loaf of bread.

Amanda kneels and gently touches his shoulder.

"Sir? Water?"

His eyes, when they fly open, look dark as a kettle. His hair, matted on one side, shines with sweat.

"Mary?" he says.

"No, sir. I'm Mrs. Carter."

"Oh, Mary, we tried to hold them off but the Yanks set up a tunnel under our lines, and tried to blow us all up. I near about lost most of my fingers. The doc said I was getting better, but now I have good reason to doubt him."

Amanda winces and holds out the cup. "Drink this if you can."

"Mary, I knew you'd come to my side." Tears spill down his cheeks, tracing lines through the grime on his face.

He tries to sit up, grimaces, then lies back. Amanda props her hand behind his head, then pours a little water in his mouth. Most of it spills out, but he swallows a little.

"I need to tell you something," he says.

"I'm so sorry, but I'm not Mary."

"I was a coward," he whispers.

"No need to say that. You were brave to get through that battle. Why don't I write a letter to Mary for you? What would you like to tell her?"

The man closes his eyes.

Amanda takes his good hand and gently says, "What's her last name? Where are you from? At least let me tell Mary I saw you."

His eyes remain closed. Amanda stands, refills the cup, and brings water to the next man.

When she leaves Mrs. Walker's, she feels wilted. Instead of

38

walking home, she heads down the 26th Street stairway and keeps going south to the river, carefully skirting Libby Prison at 20th Street. It was once a tobacco warehouse and grocery store but now it's filled with Union prisoners. She wants to avoid the guards marching outside, looking bored and bedraggled, while overheated men hoot from the windows.

She feels no need for reminders of the war right now. All she wants to see is muddy water gushing around rocks, caught up in its own momentum. A whiff of sewage indicates she's getting close to the riverbank. A train chuffs across the railroad bridge, its plume of smoke dark as a thundercloud. Maybe Jed is aboard. She imagines him propping his injured foot on the edge of a seat, his torso swaying, soot from the engine giving his hair a black sheen. The ride will be too rough for him use his sketch pad, so he will tap his long fingers against the window while he looks out. The city buildings will give way to tobacco and wheat fields, perhaps cratered by cannonballs. The trees might be fractured by bullets. Does he think of her or of his wife? What will his wife think of this maimed version of Jed? Will she become even angrier than she looks in Jed's ambrotype?

Amanda stands, hands on hips, watching the white streaks of rapids. To her left, the river roars along toward Rocketts Landing, where the Confederate Navy Yard keeps its ironclads. No one who passes on the docks can tell she is carrying a terrible secret. Just Jed and Cassie know. With one giant step, she could end her troubles. The water would close over her face, dulling the thunder of the rapids. Her body would relax into a free fall to the river bottom.

But what would become of Nell?

When Amanda was seven years old, Uncle Chester had rushed onto the porch of her parents' home, red-faced, mud on his boots. Amanda seldom saw him, though he and Aunt Margaret lived down the road. He had a gray-streaked beard and tiny arms that stuck out from a belly overstuffed as a pincushion.

"Sit down," he told Amanda, who obediently took the edge of a porch chair and swung her legs back and forth. Sally, the slave who looked after her, came out and stood behind her.

"Your parents," he said, pausing to wipe his face with a handkerchief. "You know they went into town this afternoon. Well, they were on their way home when their horse was spooked. There was a terrible accident. They have…oh, they have gone to be with God."

"Mercy!" said Sally.

"Where's God?" Amanda said.

"Why, up in heaven, of course. Didn't anyone teach you that?" said Uncle Chester.

"Then I will go to see them."

"Well, you can't go there right now. It's not your time."

"Tomorrow?"

"Not for a long time, I hope. You will come home with us."

Sally swooped down to hug Amanda, but Amanda pushed her aside and rushed upstairs to the nursery. She picked up her doll and kissed its cool, porcelain face. Just the day before, Amanda had propped the doll against a pillow in one of the chairs at the dining table while she and her mother had their afternoon tea. Later, Mummy had come upstairs to sing Amanda's favorite lullaby, "All Through the Night." When she finished, she kissed Amanda's forehead, picked up the candle and went out, her lavender scent trailing from her brocade sleeves. Now Amanda's tears dripped down, while the doll's eyes remained bright as the sapphire chips in the earrings her mother had worn.

Uncle Chester sold Sally soon after that. He put Amanda in the care of a half-blind old granny slave who sang to herself all day and barely looked at Amanda.

One day, when the granny fell asleep in her kitchen chair after giving Amanda a mug of warm milk, Amanda tiptoed through the dining room and into the greenhouse next to it. Outside, February made the landscape dun-colored, but inside the greenhouse, humid warmth pressed her cheeks and wilted the collar of her dress. Pots of plants with sprays of orange-yellow blossoms lined a shelf at the level of her shoulders. When she tilted her nose up to smell one of the flowers, a lanky man with skin the color of chestnuts stepped forward from the back of the room. He smiled at her and brushed the edge of one of the flowers with a dirt-caked finger.

"Afternoon, Missy," he said in a voice raspy like dry leaves. "You like these here pot marigolds?"

She shrugged.

He plucked off a half-dozen petals and handed them to her.

"You got a cut or a sore spot any place on you? Rub it with these and the soreness be taken away."

She wanted to rub her chest, which was stuffed with tears over the loss of her parents that she could never let out in front of anyone. Instead, she rubbed the petals on the back of her hand and inhaled a sharp, herbal scent. Then she handed the crushed bits back to him. He put them on his worktable, made from a board between two shelves of plants. Sun through the glass windows highlighted the deep creases around his eyes and mouth. His cheeks sagged like an old shirt on a clothesline, but he regarded her calmly in the sharp light. He didn't seem like he would tell her she was impertinent the way her aunt did.

"Can make tea from it, too, if you have a sore throat," he said. "Ca-len-du-la," he pronounced carefully.

"I don't," she said.

He rubbed his hands on the sides of tattered pants held up with a rope belt and turned back to the empty flowerpots on the worktable.

"Starting some peas right now. Soon as the grass brightens up, be time to move them out in the garden."

She watched as he set a saucer of peas next to the row of pots. He scooped a trowelful of dirt into each pot, placed a pea on top, then sifted dirt through his fingers to cover the pea. He motioned to her to do the same. She did, carefully lifting the pea between her thumb and forefinger. When she finished, he went to the corner of the room and brought back a watering can.

"Amanda? Where have you gotten to?" Aunt Margaret's irritated voice echoed off the greenhouse windows.

"I have to go."

"Come back. Not long from now, you see green sprouts," he promised.

She nodded and rushed back into the house, afraid Aunt Margaret would yell at her for leaving the granny slave's side. Yet her aunt didn't seem to notice what Amanda did as long as she stayed out of the way. After that, Amanda returned to the greenhouse every afternoon while Nate readied the peas and other seedlings for the garden. When the weather warmed, he brought her outside and patiently showed her how to plant and how to prune. In the fall, he explained how to expect blossoms from dirt-covered clumps that stayed underground while everything froze around them.

Around the dining table in the house, Amanda learned how to reach for the salad fork and the dinner fork at the proper times, and how to dab her lips gently with her napkin. If she tried to talk about her Mummy and Daddy, Uncle Chester looked down at his hands and Aunt Margaret said, "God's will be done. Don't dwell in the past." Amanda did as she was told, but secretly she read all the poetry books that her mother had left behind. Mummy, trained as a governess, had taught Amanda how to read, and Aunt Margaret couldn't take that away from her.

Amanda turns back to the city now. Its church spires rise up like accusing fingers. She knows what she must do.

CHAPTER TEN

Just after the gas lamps on Church Hill are lit, the carriage arrives in front of the Carter home. Betsy, Mrs. Walker's young servant, takes Nell and then hands Amanda a list of remedies that Mrs. Walker requests for her patients. Amanda pulls her bonnet low on her forehead to obscure her face. The neighbors need not see her heading out on this evening errand. She wants to wrap herself in a cloak, too, but the weather is too sultry. As she walks out, she hears a distant rumble over Oregon Hill. Perhaps another battle nears Richmond. The driver helps Amanda into the carriage. Cassie climbs nimbly into the seat next to her.

Lightning flashes before the sky erupts, pelting the roof of the carriage with rain. Amanda trembles, but Cassie sits so quietly that she seems to disappear into the seat. Only the whites of her eyes glint in the light of a passing lantern.

The rain slackens enough for Amanda to peer out as the team trots down into the congested city center. Mist lifts off the hot streets. The horses slow as they pass a hotel where carriages line up outside waiting for fares. The driver turns north, crosses Broad Street, and stops near First African Baptist Church. As he helps her down, Amanda hands him a few Confederate bills and instructs him to wait.

Cassie leads the way through the muddy street, her coffee-colored neck and arms blending into the darkness. Her quick, small steps make Amanda feel tall and gawky. People move aside for Amanda, the lone white woman in sight as they veer into an alley that smells of festering garbage. Cassie climbs two stairs and knocks at the back door of a narrow, three-story building. From the back porch, Amanda recognizes the spiky outlines of rosemary at the edge of a garden whose terraces are built of railroad ties.

A plump woman with ropy gray braids opens the door, her

wide grin revealing white teeth that seem to Amanda as large as her thumbnails. Cassie introduces the woman as Lizzie and leads Amanda into a back room. Glass jars fill floor-to-ceiling shelves, sprigs of herbs bristling from the corners. As Cassie places their wicker basket on the pine table with its smooth, sanded top, Amanda counts jars to conceal her nervousness. One, two... thirty-three.

When Lizzie asks how she can help, Amanda remembers to read Mrs. Walker's list. When she gets to willow bark, Lizzie pauses.

"Clean out of that, "says Lizzie. "All them hospitals want it."

"What you got for female trouble?" says Cassie.

"What kind of trouble?"

"About two months along, I reckon," Cassie answers.

Amanda nods, too embarrassed to speak.

"Well, then," Lizzie says, her eyes quickly darting to Amanda before she turns back to the shelf. "Tansy."

Lizzie pulls a jar off the second shelf and unscrews the lid. A gust of what smells like wet pine wafts out. "Make yourself a tea with this," she instructs as she scoops out a small handful and wraps it in cloth.

Amanda swallows, trying to tamp down her nausea.

"How it work on a body?" says Cassie.

"It get rid of the baby," says Lizzie.

Her matter-of-fact tone makes Amanda cringe. She wishes the baby would simply evaporate from her body.

"How long will it take to work?" Amanda forces herself to ask.

"A few hours. Get yourself settled tomorrow night. Not too much tea, now. Just use two or three leaves and blossoms. Liable to make a body see things, then talk out of her head..."

Amanda doesn't hear the rest. She rushes out the door and lets the dark take the nausea she has been holding back.

"...if it don't kill her first," Lizzie finishes.

CHAPTER ELEVEN

The next evening, right before dusk, Amanda goes upstairs with Nell to put her to bed instead of sending her off with Cassie. It's easy to let Cassie take charge of Nell, but Amanda sometimes feels left out of their easy rapport. The girl's thin arms reach up and clasp Amanda's neck. Her skin smells like the sage leaves she picked in the garden that afternoon.

Amanda brushes the curls back from Nell's forehead. The little girl's hairline is damp and slightly sticky. She needs to tell Cassie to wash her face more thoroughly.

Amanda traces one finger over each of Nell's cheeks. Nell giggles.

"That tickles, Mama!"

Amanda smiles and resolves to spend more time with her daughter after the tansy puts these troubles behind her. She wishes Nell had more space around her in which to play. The house and garden seem so confining compared to the gardens and rolling tobacco fields of Amelia County. Not knowing any-thing different, Nell contentedly goes in and out of the back door, carrying her doll and humming to herself.

Amanda begins to sing a lullaby. "Sleep my child, and peace attend thee…" she begins, and pauses because her voice shakes at the vivid memory of her Mummy singing those words as she put Amanda to bed the night before she was killed.

"Sing more," says Nell, and Amanda makes herself contin-ue, wiping her eyes with the back of her hand.

How little Amanda remembers of her Mummy, who came from England, which she called "the land over the sea." Riding in her arms, Amanda felt like she was rocking on a boat, even though she had never seen the wide, wave-tossed water that her mother talked about. Mummy had behaved improperly, too, but it turned out all right because Amanda's father agreed to marry her. How disappointed she would be to see Amanda now.

When Amanda walks downstairs, she sees that Cassie has already laid old sheets on the parlor rug. Amanda doesn't want to lie on the sofa and risk staining it. The pallet reminds her of the first time she saw Jed when he was immobilized, his eyes clouded with pain.

She momentarily considers telling Cassie to dump the tansy down the privy and put away the linens. She has refused to dwell on the possibility of overdose, but now she imagines herself pale and rigid on the pallet like one of the soldiers who has to be carried out by Mrs. Walker's manservant. Rubbing her hands along her waist, Amanda urges herself to see the tansy as a tonic, cleaning her out. She will rise from the pallet pale but restored to the good health that she needs in order to attend to her responsibilities as Nell's mother and as a wife patiently waiting for her husband to return.

In the kitchen, Cassie has unwrapped Lizzie's packet and spread the yellow flowers and spiky leaves on top of the table. Nate taught Amanda about pot marigolds, Indian tobacco, and other plants that could be used as medicines, but he never showed her tansy. Maybe he knew nothing about it, or he left it up to some of the slave women to grow in their quarters where Amanda was forbidden to go.

"Ready, Missus?" says Cassie, facing the pot of boiling water so Amanda can't see her expression. "Lizzie be along soon, before dark."

Amanda bites her bottom lip, trying not to let the tansy odor bother her, and nods. Sweat already dampens the neck of the old chemise that she plans to burn in the stove when this is done. Cassie places two blossoms and three leaves in a white cup painted with roses, the one that belonged to Amanda's mother, then pours in the water. She sets the cup and saucer on a tray and carries it into the parlor. Amanda follows.

"Ought to sit," says Cassie, putting down the cup and gesturing toward the sofa.

"Yes. My last chance to be civilized," says Amanda with a rueful smile. Cassie hands her one of the old sheets to put underneath herself before she settles with an embroidered pillow behind her back. Raising the cup to her lips, Amanda pretends she is daintily sipping during one of her aunt's genteel afternoon teas until she tastes the bitter brew. Her mouth wrinkles, but she manages to swallow once, then again. She sits back and closes her eyes.

When she opens them again, Lizzie looms over the sofa. She gives Amanda a long, searching look and asks, "When you drink?"

"Just a little while ago."

"Give it time."

Cassie helps Amanda down onto the pallet and goes into the kitchen with Lizzie. A burst of laughter occasionally punctuates their murmuring. Lizzie will stay the night. Negroes, even free ones, are not allowed to be out after dark.

Amanda closes her eyes and hears Aunt Margaret scold her for coming out of her bedroom so late at night. She tells her aunt that her room is drafty and cold, and she's warming her feet by what's left of the fire. What she doesn't say is that if she waits long enough, a figure in a peacock-blue dress might flash past, calling for her. "Mandy? Oh, Mandy!" And she will always answer, "Mummy!"

"Go to bed, you crazy child," says Aunt Margaret, her blonde hair trailing down her back like icicles.

Amanda opens her eyes and looks around. She knows she should roll over onto her back, but it's so hard to make her arms and legs work. Her whole body feels heavy. She closes her eyes again.

In her next hallucination, she feels Jed brushing his hand across her nipple. She leans against him, gently touching his thigh. They wrap their arms around each other, but then Jed abruptly pushes her away. He stands, his foot suddenly healed, lifting her and running through the garden gate, both of them scandalously bare, out for anyone to see. Then he's running so fast that they lift off, flying over the exhausted city, now side by side, two birds who can swoop and soar anywhere. Below, Edwin shouts and points up at them, holding Nell.

A cramp makes Amanda cry out. Lizzie comes in, rubs Amanda's face with a soft cloth, and gently pushes Amanda's gown up to check for bleeding. She sees none. Amanda alternately wakes, cramps, and sleeps.

At dawn, Cassie tiptoes past Amanda, still asleep in the corner of the parlor, and covers her with a sheet. Lizzie checks on her too, gently moving aside her legs, and sees a pale sheet beneath her.

"Baby still with her. That happen sometimes," says Lizzie matter-of-factly.

"She need more tea?" asks Cassie.

"Not if she want to stay here on this earth."

Cassie exhales softly. "Trouble just beginning for her."

CHAPTER TWELVE

Pulling the brush through Nell's curls, Cassie remembers fixing her daughter's hair. She had to work one section at a time, pulling it up and then braiding it tight. The two of them sat on the steps behind the Scruggs's kitchen, after she had washed and stacked their supper dishes. Julia rested her head against her mother's knees as Cassie hummed and tried not to pull too hard. The girl's hair had a little kink to it. Her skin, the color of tea with lots of milk, and the greenish tint to her eyes, made her look like Clancy. Running her fingers along Julia's scalp felt as sustaining as working the sun-warmed soil for the little garden she and Clancy kept behind the stable.

Cassie wonders how Julia wears her hair now. When Cassie was sold away, Julia was about eight years old. She would be a young woman by now. Is she practical, covering her head with a scarf the way Cassie does? Or does she still wear the two shoulder-length braids the way she did when Cassie left in the wagon with Master Scruggs?

Cassie's departure took place with stunning swiftness a few days after Miss Mildred's wedding. Master Scruggs came into the kitchen following the noontime meal and told Cassie she would be going to Richmond that afternoon.

"Master and Missus Carter sent for you. Their new girl won't do. They're selling her."

Cassie set down the dishpan and dried her hands.

"But…" she began.

"No questions," he said. The overseer stepped in behind him. The doorway silhouetted his bulk. "No trouble."

The overseer followed her as she slipped into her room behind the pantry to roll her extra dress and headscarf into a bundle. Her hands felt numb. She kept her other belongings in the room above the stable. If she was allowed to get those, maybe she could try to signal Clancy and at least glimpse Julia, who was weeding the Scruggs's vegetable garden, and Gabriel, who was down at the quarters with the granny who took care of all the young slave children. This was the way they sold slaves here—no warnings, no goodbyes. Since she had an important job in the house, she had never expected to be one of those sold. If she ran outside or started hollering and carrying on, they would whip and gag her. Words boiled in her throat.

"My young'uns…" she began again.

The overseer backhanded her across the mouth.

"Pack some food," he ordered.

Her mouth throbbed. Silently, she heaped biscuits into a sack, cut a slab of smoked ham, and picked out six of the first apples of the fall crop. It was a Saturday, the one night she was allowed to spend with Clancy and the children in his room above the stable. No matter now, she thought bitterly. She kept her head down and refused to look anywhere but at her callused feet as the overseer pushed her to the wagon.

When she did look up to climb into the back, she saw Clancy at the head of the team of horses, one hand on the reins, the other on his hat brim. He removed his hat, caught her eye, and gave her a searing look that telegraphed his hurt and her need to be strong. When he bowed his head, his light brown neck gleamed with sweat.

Her tears dropped like beads that came unstrung.

As Master Scruggs drove the wagon away, Julia rushed up from the quarters, Gabriel beside her. Gabriel was just three and couldn't go much farther than the row of linden trees bordering the front lane. He called, "Mama, Mama!" Julia ran into the lane, waving and wailing until the overseer caught up to her and yanked her arm so hard she lost her balance and fell in the road.

As Cassie curled her body into a tight arc, she felt in her apron pocket and found Julia's hair ribbon. It was a deep aubergine color, a scrap from one of Missus Scruggs's dresses. She wrapped the ribbon so tightly that her fingers turned pale as the wheels bounced over the ruts.

Now Cassie ties a yellow ribbon around the top of Miss Nell's head, then stands back with her hands on her hips.

"Pretty," Nell says, patting the ribbon.

"Leave it be, now," says Cassie, holding out her hand to lead the girl downstairs.

Cassie thinks about the tasks ahead of her. It's wash day, and dangerous for Nell to be near the big kettles of boiling water. Missus Carter used to take the girl out for walks to distract her, but Missus is always feeling raggedy and stays in bed much of the morning. God has a plan for Missus, surely, in keeping her from getting rid of that baby, but Cassie wonders what it is.

In the dining room, Cassie pulls out Miss Nell's chair and tells her to wait for breakfast. Next, Cassie goes to the well. Nell gets up and follows her out the kitchen door. Cassie sighs. There's no point in scolding her when the girl just wants someone to pay attention to her. Nell trails along as Cassie brings in water, lights the stove, and sets up a pot of water to boil. After it boils, she slowly stirs in cornmeal. To help Nell be patient and wait until the mush is cool enough to eat, she starts a clapping game—one clap, which Nell repeats, then two, then three.

After she serves Nell at the kitchen table, Cassie darts into the pantry and pulls a small sack from behind the cooking pots. Just a handful of coffee beans remains from a hoard that Lizzie gave her at Christmas. Cassie keeps this supply hidden from Missus and makes a cup only when Missus won't notice and take the rest of the beans for herself.

Cassie sips, remembering how Clancy came by the kitchen on the mornings when he hitched up the team of horses and waited to take Master or Missus Scruggs to town. How lucky they both felt for an extra moment together. If no one was looking, he kissed her, his lips warm, his breath scented with the coffee she served him from one of the chipped earthenware mugs given to slaves to use. She wants to return to the simple pleasure of standing next to her husband in the kitchen, knowing their children are nearby.

The coffee sinks down, warming Cassie as Nell asks for more food.

CHAPTER THIRTEEN

Amanda leans over the polished walnut lap desk in her bedroom and tries to answer Edwin's letter. Paper is in short supply, and she has already ripped up three precious sheets. The pen slides in her sweaty hand. Aunt Margaret had her friend stop by occasionally to teach Amanda ladylike penmanship, but Amanda's handwriting sprawls like a morning glory vine. With a sigh, she begins again. She thought the tansy would wash everything away and there would be nothing to hide. Now every word mocks her.

It was with surprise and gratitude that I received your letter telling me of your illness and your recovery, she writes.

"Panic, too," she thinks. She crosses out the word surprise. With all these cross-outs, she will have to copy the letter onto yet another clean sheet of paper.

I am grateful that you have recovered your health, she begins again. No, that sounds too formal. Closing her eyes, Amanda wonders if she ever really knew what to say to Edwin. She remembers their first breakfast at the dining room table in Richmond. After waking next to Edwin's still unfamiliar body, Amanda slipped down to the outhouse, embarrassed that he might hear her pissing in the chamber pot. She lingered in the garden, breathing in sage-scented air and planning where the first rows of parsley and thyme would go. When she walked back through the dining room, Edwin was already dressed and sitting in the chair that faced the china cabinet. He wore dark pants and a waistcoat, the marks of a wet comb in his chestnut hair. In a little while, he would go down the hill to his Carter Tobacco warehouse in Shockoe Valley. Still in her dressing gown, loose hair like a tangle of pachysandra, Amanda felt confused about what to do next. Should she dress first or sit with him? Uncle Chester and Aunt Margaret always came down for breakfast together. They orbited and intersected with each other all day like they were part of a quadrille. Amanda wondered what she should talk about. Uncle Chester always had a word about the crops at the breakfast table, but there was no tobacco growing in Richmond.

Edwin gestured for her to sit down. As Cassie poured coffee, Amanda picked up *The Richmond Daily Dispatch*. Crenshaw's store advertised a new shipment of silks and organdies. She folded the paper and set it down. Edwin picked it up and began scanning the news about John Letcher's election as Virginia's new governor. The wallpaper, a fading vine and leaf pattern that Edwin's first wife must have chosen, depressed Amanda. So did the mauve curtains. It would be so much cheerier if she could see the garden through the windows.

"I was thinking," Amanda said carefully, gauging Edwin's reaction.

He used a forefinger to pull his eyeglasses down his nose for a better look at her.

"This room could benefit from some new drapes. I'd like to go shopping for fabric today."

He shrugged. "You may do that. Use my charge account at Crenshaw's. Cassie will go with you to show you the way."

"Do you have a favorite color?"

He shrugged again. "Anything you choose, that's fine with me."

"What are you finding in the newspaper?" she tried again.

"Politics. Our new governor brooks no loyalty to the South. He's for the Union, it seems."

"Tell me more," said Amanda, who had overheard Uncle Chester railing against the abolitionist agitators and other scoundrels from the North, though Amanda had not paid much attention at the time.

Edwin waved a hand dismissively. "No concern of yours right now. Take care of the curtains and the garden."

Amanda bit her lip. Lonely hours, filled with bolts of fabric and wet dirt, stretched before her once again.

He finished his coffee, lit his pipe, and vanished in a wreath of smoke. Maybe that was the beginning of the distance between them.

Today, when the light softens into late afternoon, Amanda copies her best sentences onto a fresh sheet of paper. If she keeps the letter short, she won't sound so false-hearted.

> *June 18, 1864*
> *Dear Edwin,*
>
> *Oh, what wonderful news your letter brought! It had been so long since I heard from you that I truly feared the worst. I expect this letter will find you already on the march again leading a new regiment, so I send it in haste in the hope that it will catch up with you before you have moved too far and that someone there will know where to find you.*
>
> *All is well here. The beans and cucumbers are growing so well that I've plenty to share with Mrs. Walker and the men at her wayside. Nell cheers us up by scampering to and fro in the garden. We can sometimes hear cannon fire close to Richmond, but nothing has reached us yet. We are all safe and send you love. Please send news soon again.*
> *Affectionately,*
> *Amanda*

Then she goes out back, where Cassie is bringing in laundry from the clothesline, to tell her she is taking Nell for a walk. She will post the letter in the morning.

"You up to this so soon?" says Cassie. Amanda had taken the tansy just three days ago.

Amanda smiles brightly, falsely. "Nothing more to do."

Nell runs out from behind a sheet, clapping her hands. Amanda vows to take the girl out more often. The outings will be a distraction. Soon enough, Amanda's condition will force her to stay indoors.

She opens the gate, nodding to a neighbor dressed in black, the color of mourning, now ubiquitous in the city. Nell's head comes up to Amanda's waist. Cassie has remade one of Amanda's old beige dresses into the right size for Nell. Amanda wishes she could buy fabric for a new dress that would match Nell's yellow hair ribbon, but the mills in England and up north no longer send newly woven cloth to the South.

As they walk down East Grace Street, the light lengthens their shadows into two enormous heads with bulbous skirts underneath. Nell lags behind, kicking stones and singing to herself. Amanda walks up the block towards St. John's Church so they can enjoy the shade of its yard for a few minutes. She craves the breeze and the quiet paths above Grace Street. As they near the building, one of Richmond's oldest churches, she sees that the white paint on its clapboards looks grimy. Weeds sprout in back of the gravestones. With the war on, nobody has time for upkeep anymore. The free Negro men usually hired to do gardening are now forced to build fortifications for Richmond. By the time Amanda and Nell climb the stairs leading into the churchyard, Amanda is exasperated by their slow progress. She sits on a bench while Nell, arms open, chases a white cabbage butterfly.

Up the hill behind the church stands a general hospital in a former tobacco warehouse, taking up an entire city block. Two nuns from the Sisters of Charity emerge from the front entrance and slowly make their way down the steps, carrying armloads of folded sheets. She seldom sees the Sisters outdoors, as their mission keeps them inside the hospital wards. From this distance, their wimples look like wings. They also run St. Joseph's Villa for orphaned girls on Fourth Street, down in the center of Richmond. Could they somehow remove her from her troubles, sheltering her among them until she gives birth and then giving her baby to another family afterwards?

The woods and fields of Richmond's outskirts rise into gentle hills at the horizon. Amanda watches her daughter circle in front of her, arms still stretched wide, the butterfly weaving its way in and out of them, eluding capture. When Nell returns to Amanda, out of breath, Amanda smiles and opens her arms but still watches the nuns, wondering how to approach them in the strictest of confidence.

CHAPTER FOURTEEN

The day brings weather steamy enough to make the edges of the *Daily Dispatch* curl. While Cassie goes to the cistern with Nell to fill buckets for watering the drooping vegetables, Amanda reads about the evacuation of Atlanta. Houses torn to pieces. People going about with bags of plunder. Yankee camps outfitted with parlor chairs and fine feather pillows. Amanda puts her teacup back in its saucer and wonders what it would feel like to have soldiers carry off the very chair she sits in. Filthy, greedy men, she thinks.

All the fighting under the "War News" is beginning to sound the same to her. Attacks. Bloody repulses. Enemy pursued. Roads torn, trestlework burned. Severe losses. Troops withdrawn. Artillery captured. Yet a lull in the fighting sounds ominous, too. "Everything is painfully quiet below, for the deeper the sleep the more startling the awakening. We shall doubtless hear something shortly," the paper announced one day in its report from Petersburg.

She wonders if Edwin might be caught up in the next deadly volleys there. She has not heard from him again since she sent her reply. Has he been reassigned yet? Perhaps he lies on his belly in a trench, sweat-soaked and filthy. He lifts his head to fire his rifle, then wriggles back down out of danger. He could die heroically, never suspecting her betrayal. Then she chastises herself for these thoughts. What did he do to deserve such a fate?

Amanda goes out to the back porch and watches as Cassie bends over the row of tomatoes, pulling out weeds and creating a small pile by her feet. She hands Nell the long stems she uproots. Nell carefully twists them together and announces to Cassie that she's making a nest for the birds. Cassie stops to show her how to shape the stems into a bowl. Together, they go to the magnolia tree, pick out a branch, and carefully balance the nest against the trunk.

As they walk back to the rows of vegetables, Cassie says, "Don't be expecting a mama bird to fly on in there and set down her eggs. That's a springtime thing. And most mama birds build nests their own selves."

"But a mama bird can sit there if she wants to."

Cassie nods.

Amanda wishes she had Cassie's natural touch with Nell. If Nell told her she wanted to make a nest, Amanda would probably say there was no use in doing so, and make her take the weeds to the pile at the back of the garden where they belonged.

She wonders about Cassie's children. Do they have her compact efficiency, or do they take after her husband, whoever he is? How old are they now? What if Amanda sent for them so they could at least visit their mother? Yet such a request would be highly irregular, especially from Edwin's new wife. The only way the children could really see their mother is if Master Scruggs agreed to sell them to the Carters, and Edwin would never approve of that.

During her first year in Richmond, Amanda had asked Edwin if he might consider buying Nate from her aunt and uncle. She missed seeing him every day and wanted to give him a peaceful place to spend his final years. Edwin said, "Our place is too small for a gardener. Besides, he's too old to do any heavy work. He's better off where he is."

Amanda remembered Nate working in the camellia bed, a stained straw hat shading his face as he squatted with his clippers. Pink blossoms piled up next to his foot.

"Why do you have to cut them so much?" she had said.

"Cut now, they grow back strong in spring."

"But it's so cruel."

"A broken place, it can heal up. Flowers be even prettier next time they come up."

Amanda exchanged letters with Aunt Margaret a few times after she moved to Richmond. In one, she asked about Nate. Aunt Margaret wrote back and said, "You need to occupy yourself with your husband and daughter, and no longer concern yourself with the servants here. The old man you asked about, Nate, took sick and died this winter."

Aunt Margaret would easily replace Nate with a young, strong boy from the slave quarters. Amanda silently mourned Nate's loss, afraid to tell Edwin because he wouldn't understand why a slave mattered so much to her. After that, she felt even more distant from her aunt and uncle's house—and from Edwin.

Now Amanda makes herself go back inside and return to the newspaper. There's no use thinking about what happens to slaves who belong to others. It's beyond her control.

After Cassie finishes in the garden, Amanda says it's time that they set out for First Market. Amanda decides to avoid visiting the dry goods stores on Main Street because it depresses her to see the shelves so depleted. Once stocked with cloth in every color from forsythia to chartreuse, the stores now specialize in black for all the grieving women. Right after she and Edwin married, Amanda proudly shopped for silk for a new dress to wear to the theater. She chose a cream-colored moiré, which set off the blue in her eyes, and a wool shawl. How elegant she felt on Edwin's arm as they strolled under the gaslights, the soft hiss and sputtering glow making her feel like she was the one walking onto the stage.

Edwin's foreman from Carter Tobacco still occasionally stops by with cash, but it's hard to keep enough on hand. At first Edwin sent home part of his salary, but he is no longer regularly paid. Prices have become so inflated that it takes a wad of Confederate bills to buy one item. Even though two mills are right in town, flour can sell as high as $230 or $275 per barrel. Cornmeal is easier to come by, but still $40 per bushel. All Amanda can afford is five or six cups at a time. She can't remember the last time she was able to find bacon or fresh eggs, two provisions always in ample supply before the war.

Nell skips ahead, kicking an acorn. When the acorn skitters under a handcart, she stops.

"Mama, I want a raisin cake," she says.

"A raisin cake?" Amanda repeats, and then laughs. "I haven't seen one of those since you were a bitty thing!"

Nell scowls. "I want one!"

"Not today. We'll be lucky to find a cup of flour so Cassie can make you a biscuit."

Cassie shakes her head. "Before long, I be making biscuits out of mashed-up acorns."

"Ewww!" says Nell. "Squirrels eat acorns."

"I'm ready to eat some meat, but not a squirrel," says Amanda, whose appetite is finally starting to return.

At that, Nell wrinkles up her nose and rushes ahead. She picks up a stick and drags it behind her. Hardly any other shoppers walk past them. Amanda doesn't blame them for staying home. Everyone who goes to the market comes home in a bad mood.

Amanda, Cassie, and Nell pass a fruit stand displaying shriveled apples. A group of boys circles beside it yelling, "Stone the Yankee!" They hurl pebbles at another boy who hastily ducks behind a wagon and yells back, "I ain't no Yankee!"

Amanda pulls Nell close.

As they climb back up from Main Street with two pounds of cornmeal, a pound of flour, and a cup of sorghum syrup, the sky darkens. When they are a block away from home, the clouds open, soaking their hair and splashing mud up onto their dresses. Cassie hugs the tote sack against her chest so the flour and cornmeal don't get wet.

After Cassie dries Nell and settles her on the couch with a picture book, she comes upstairs to take Amanda's wet clothes. She will hang them on the line in the yard when it stops raining.

Amanda has dropped her dress on the floor and is stepping out of her soggy petticoats. She waits for Cassie to loosen her corset and help pull it over her head. Cassie glances at the slight curve in Amanda's belly and then looks away. Rain streams down the windows.

"Cassie?" says Amanda, rubbing her wet face with a towel, "didn't you want to find a man after you came here? Someone at church? If you got married again, you could have visiting privileges, you know."

Cassie looks out the window at the dripping magnolia leaves. Visiting privileges meant that slaves who were married but owned by two different masters could visit one another as long as they carried passes and obeyed curfews and other laws.

"No need of a man."

"Is your husband at the Scruggs's place?"

"Probably still there, caring for horses—unless he sold off, too."

"Why not write to him?" Amanda blurts out without thinking.

Cassie stares at her, eyes glittering like jagged fragments of glass.

"No, of course not," says Amanda. She flushes, embarrassed. All her life, she has known that slaves are not allowed to learn to read or write. "This baby is making me lose my head."

Amanda goes to the wardrobe and picks out a dry dress and petticoat, her back to Cassie.

"Soon, my clothes won't fit me," she muses.

Cassie waits, the wet clothes in a pile by her bare feet.

"Where will I go?" Amanda continues. "I'll be stuck in the house and in the garden all day, every day. Nobody can see me like this. I'll have to tell Mrs. Walker I'm too ill to come back and help her."

"What you telling Master Carter?" says Cassie.

Amanda sighs. "Nothing."

"If he come home? What then?"

"I don't know," she says, sitting on the edge of the bed and putting her face in her hands. Her voice is muffled as she repeats, "I just don't know."

Then she looks up. "I think the Sisters of Charity could help me. They could take me in."

"And Miss Nell?"

"You'd take care of her."

Cassie looks out the window so long that Amanda wonders if she heard her. Finally, Cassie says, "Why leave now? Master Carter still gone."

With one finger, Amanda traces the patterns in the lace on the bedspread. "But he could come back."

"Go to the Sisters if he do."

Amanda considers this as Cassie leans over to pick up the wet clothes. Cassie sounds so sensible, but is it right to keep taking advice about such an important matter from her slave?

"But what if he surprises me?"

Cassie shrugs. "You got time to think on that. Baby won't be here 'til winter. You have some kin you could visit?"

"My aunt? She has no children of her own. She never wanted me there in the first place," says Amanda, tears springing forth. She quickly wipes them away with the back of her hand. Cassie doesn't need to know how forsaken she felt there.

"Any other folks?"

Amanda shakes her head.

Cassie puts the wet clothes back on the floor, goes to the bureau, and hands Amanda a handkerchief. "Then you best off staying here," Cassie says.

CHAPTER FIFTEEN

Shouting startles Cassie from her pallet. She quickly slips her dress over her head and heads into the kitchen to peer out the back door. Crickets rasp in the muggy air.

"You dad-blamed son of a bitch!" someone hollers on the other side of the garden wall.

Cassie dares not open the back gate to investigate because the men might turn their rage against her. She climbs onto the cistern and peers over the wall. The moon spotlights two drunken soldiers fighting. The tall one with shirttails dangling from his pants gut-punches the short one who has lost his hat. A thud follows, and the tall one rushes away.

"Let them all kill each other," she thinks as she climbs down. In the early days of the war, the newly enlisted Confederate soldiers swaggered through the Richmond streets with an unholy racket of drums. Their rifle muskets poked up into the Lord's face. These days, they look like heaps of rags being hauled on stretchers from the train depot to the receiving hospitals.

The short man slumps against the wall. Piss soaks the front of his pants and the ground underneath. His skin is the color of the soapy scum in laundry water.

"God's will be done," she whispers, then spits at him before climbing down. She hopes he will be gone by the time it's light outside, as Missus Carter may decide to help him.

Instead of going back into her room, Cassie slowly navigates the pathway between the vegetable rows to the rear of the garden, her arms stretched in front of her to keep spider's webs from her face. Moonlight guides her. She makes her way behind the heap of weeds and kitchen scraps, where she keeps a secret stash of vegetables. She doesn't want the soldiers at Missus Walker's to feast on the best of the garden. If she could, she'd take all the vegetables destined for the soldiers down the hill to the slave pens in Lumpkin's Jail, a stockade in the swampy mire of Shockoe Creek. Traders in too-fancy suits prowl around there. They would sooner throw Cassie into the jail and sell her off than let her make a delivery to aid the slaves.

She picks up a tomato and settles down on the bench, defying the rule that forbids her from using the same seats as the Carters or any white people. She leans forward and bites into the tomato, letting its juice fall to the ground instead of onto her dress. After she finishes, she wipes her hands on the ground and leans back, luxuriating in the forbidden comfort.

Even though the Scruggs's property was much larger than the Carter garden, she could never walk around like this when she lived there. Between the Scruggs family and the other slaves, too many people tracked her every move. She walked in a prescribed triangle from the big house to Clancy's room above the stable to the slave cabin where the granny too old to keep working in the tobacco fields looked after her children.

The first year she and Clancy took up together, one night, he carried her into the far field and made a blanket of his shirt. He wasn't much taller than she was, with a compact body made strong by bridling and leading horses. The bright August moon seemed to shatter the rules about where they were allowed to be at night. His pale brown skin glowed almost white. Her eyes felt sticky in the humidity.

"It ain't right, having to steal away like this, just to be with my woman," whispered Clancy, lying down next to her. He stroked her hips.

Cassie looked up at each star wavering in the blackness. She traced lines down his bare chest before she pulled off her dress.

"We do what we want when nobody looking," she said. "Just got to wait for the right time."

Now Cassie closes her eyes and prays for a sign about what she might do next. Missus Carter treats her well enough, as long as she keeps up with her work. But Missus hasn't been the same since that soldier came and went. The Lord clearly did not want the baby to be taken from Missus. Does He have a plan for Cassie, too?

A light breeze stirs the leaves. When Cassie opens her eyes, darkness under the crape myrtle trees surrounds her without texture. She imagines gathering the darkness in her hands like a length of velvet and sewing it into a soft, hooded cloak for herself, too fine for a slave woman to wear. In this cloak, she picks up a white baby and carries him in her arms through nights and days, over rocks and running water. At the end of the journey stands a cradle surrounded by voile. She parts the voile, gently places the baby in the cradle, and walks away. The baby cries for Cassie to return, but Cassie keeps walking, her steps light and sure. Behind her, she hears another woman's voice soothing the baby.

As the horizon begins to streak with pink, Cassie stands, wondering when the Lord will call on her to fulfill the plan He has shown her. The soldier is still passed out below. She trudges to the well and pulls up the day's first bucket of water.

CHAPTER SIXTEEN

Amanda feels a burst of energy now that September has brought cooler weather and her sickness has lifted. Wearing a light shawl to camouflage her thickening waist, she strolls east down Grace Street, inhaling the wet tobacco scent drifting up from the few manufacturers still operating in Shockoe Valley. The Carter Tobacco warehouse that Edwin owns is down there, too, stockpiling whatever part of the harvest his brother and other growers in central Virginia can manage to send. The market for tobacco has collapsed during the war, but it could return. She walks by herself, too restless today to keep Nell's pace.

The maples are tinged with red and orange, adding a touch of color to the muted brick and stone buildings. Black crepe flutters from many doorways, heralding yet another soldier's death. She dreads the upcoming months of hiding from Mrs. Walker and everyone else.

Edwin wrote that he continues under the command of General Jubal Early, but was reassigned to the western part of Virginia, out in the Blue Ridge Mountains near Winchester. The *Daily Dispatch* describes his main opponent, General Philip Sheridan, as a cruel man who directs his Yankee troops to generally devastate the country, "sparing neither houses, barns, stock, grain, nor anything else." Yet in his most recent letter, Edwin seemed to be making the best of the situation.

> *September 8, 1864*
> *My Dear Wife,*
> *I hope this letter finds you and Nell in good health. We went through Winchester a few days ago, which looks badly devastated from previous fighting, but we are now in camp near Berryville and fairly well provisioned from nearby farms. Some of the men and I gathered a few apples but they*

were too sour and worm-eaten to be of much use. We fill the days with drills and the nights with cards. I won a little tobacco with which to fill my pipe. To think, my warehouse used to unload tobacco from train cars by the barrelful.

Well, we are mostly in good spirits and glad of the respite from constantly moving around. Some of the men are on a raiding party on the B&O railroad, but we remain here to defend this portion of the Valley should the relentless enemy decide to advance in this direction.

In your last letter, you told me of all the shortages. Things must be a little better now with all the supplements from the vegetable garden, I expect. Richmond should be well protected, with defenses ringing the city on both sides of the James River. Give Nell a kiss for me. I send you a kiss, too.

Your ever loving,
Edwin

So far, Amanda has kept her letters brief and focused on little stories about Nell and the daily challenge of finding food, or washing soda, quicklime, and other household supplies. It's the least she can do to lift his spirits and keep him from suspecting anything. The *Daily Dispatch* reports that news from General Early is encouraging, with the enemy "falling back down the Valley." Edwin is safe for now, and still far away.

There is little progress in the war on other fronts. Union General Sherman remains in Atlanta while Georgia's governor sets aside September 15 as a day of fasting and prayer. Petersburg has been quiet except for a bit of shelling.

How different the news sounded in the spring of 1861. On April 17, the night that the Virginia Convention voted to secede from the Union, people rushed with torches past the Carter home. Edwin went out on the porch, then motioned for Amanda to join him. It was understood that she would leave Nell with Cassie. Edwin and Amanda liked to stroll together after dinner, but this night, his broad strides left her breathless as they followed the lights to Capitol Square. When they reached the lawn of the capitol, Amanda tightened her grip on Edwin's elbow and pointed. A Confederate flag fluttered above the white columns of the building's portico. The swath of red fabric with its cross of stars set in blue swirled in the sky like wine in a goblet.

"What a welcome sight," Edwin said. "Soon Mr. Lincoln won't be able to tell me how to run my warehouse or tell my brother how to grow our tobacco."

Amanda said nothing. In the torchlight, wind looked like it was gusting through Edwin's wheat-colored eyes.

The first shot in a hundred-gun salute to the Confederate states startled Amanda. The mosaic of flames from the torches and the men's dark hats made her nervous. Even though she had lived in Richmond for two years, she still had not grown accustomed to crowds. She clung to Edwin's arm as he cheered. Secession sounded like such a glorious, high-minded word, but what would it mean every day? She couldn't imagine living anywhere but in Virginia, yet Abraham Lincoln's call to raise an army to fight the secessionists sounded ominous. Her home state would be swept up in the military actions that had started in South Carolina.

"Edwin, let's go home," she had said.

"Where's your patriotism, Mrs. Carter? A time like this only comes along once."

Amanda had never seen him so animated. He usually measured his words before speaking the way he measured tobacco between his thumb and forefinger before filling the bowl of his pipe and tamping it down. His broad cheeks had turned ruddy, his face a mask of fervor. The torches backlit his shoulders, making it seem like he towered over her.

She dared not ask again to go home. Relinquishing his arm, she dug her shoes into the new grass on the lawn as he clapped, until stars emerged over the triangular roof of the capitol and the crowd dispersed. As they trudged back up Main Street, she walked silently one pace behind, nervous and resentful of his excitement, as he hummed the "La Marseillaise."

As Amanda walks now, reversing the route that she and Edwin had taken in 1861, she passes the home of "Crazy Bet" Van Lew, who dares to bring food to the Union officers at Libby Prison. What would it be like to so openly defy the Southern Cause? The Van Lew home looks perfectly respectable, with fallen leaves raked from its yard and the balustrade that fronts the uppermost windows coated in fresh-looking white paint. Nonetheless, Bet goes around talking to herself, not one whit concerned about what others think. Amanda wishes she had that kind of insouciance so she could continue to go through the streets as her pregnancy begins to show. Yet that wouldn't be fair to Edwin's good reputation as a businessman.

The street ends in a bluff. Chimneys, sloped roofs, and white-trimmed dormer windows line Shockoe Valley. The commotion of horses and wagons in the streets sounds like an insignificant drone from here. She feels no connection to the city below, nor to the capitol on the hill that rises out of the haze, where politicians argue all day and all night in the Confederate legislature. They discuss how they will keep paying for the war, and whether they should even continue meeting in the Virginia state capitol building or find another accommodation. Amanda's concerns are more personal and immediate.

Instead of returning home, Amanda goes right to Mrs. Walker's house. There isn't anything to bring from the garden today. She and Cassie picked most of the tomatoes, and the turnips and carrots could use more time to fatten underground before being harvested. Lucy shows her into the parlor. Mrs. Walker wears a rose-colored dress with lace trim around its sleeves. She sits alone in the lady's chair, all the men out in the garden or on their pallets. The skin underneath her eyes looks dark as a bruise, surrounded by a pale and waxy complexion.

Reverend Walker, absorbed with his own ministry, has taken to sleeping most nights at the church, leaving her with the entire responsibility of the hospital.

Mrs. Walker folds bandages and motions for Amanda to help. Amanda picks up a big stack, which slides onto the floor as she sits on the sofa. When she leans over to retrieve the pile, she feels off kilter with her head down. Her swollen stomach prevents her from sitting up straight again without assistance.

"Oh, child, what is wrong?" says Mrs. Walker, getting up and putting out her arm to help.

As Amanda rights herself, sound and light fade. Then everything goes black.

When she opens her eyes again, she lies on the sofa, her corset loosened. Betsy holds a cold towel against her forehead. Mrs. Walker frowns, her forehead like a balled-up sheet of paper. Her icy eyes dart down to Amanda's waist.

"Mrs. Carter, I believe I know the source of your troubles," she says.

Amanda closes her eyes and braces herself for the condemnation that is sure to follow.

"Ye adulterers and adulteresses, know ye not that the friendship of the world is enmity with God? Whosoever therefore will be a friend of the world is the enemy of God," Mrs. Walker intones.

Amanda feels her cheeks flaming. What a fool she was to think she could continue playing the charade of the charitable soldier's wife helping the poor, wounded men. She had planned to leave on good terms in just a week or two, telling Mrs. Walker that she was feeling poorly—she thought she had an ague—and could not continue to help at the hospital until she regained her strength. Now Mrs. Walker is banishing her with ignominy.

"The Reverend and I run a decent, Christian hospital here. You have greatly helped and comforted the men. You have brought them the bounty of your garden. For this, I give thanks. But now," she stops to take in a deep breath, "you must not affront us with the evidence of your wanton ways."

Amanda says nothing, tears sliding down her cheeks and into her ears.

"I have no need of you nor your bastard child in the making. You must go. Now!"

Amanda tries to blink away the black spots from her vision.

"See her to the door," Mrs. Walker says to Betsy.

With that, Mrs. Walker turns her back and rushes out of the room.

Betsy's long arms poke out from the sleeves of her gray, crudely stitched homespun dress. She brings one hand in front of her mouth as if to hide a smirk when she asks Amanda if she needs help standing. Amanda wills herself to push up from the sofa and propel herself out of this horrid room, which reeks of putrefaction. Yet when she starts to walk, she has to take Betsy's hand to steady herself.

Out on Franklin Street, Amanda hesitates, dazed, one hand on an iron fence post, but sends Betsy back into Mrs. Walker's house. There's no need for further humiliation. Raindrops, just beginning to fall, thump the top of her head. Two neighbors hurry past, their hoop skirts swaying like foxglove blossoms. How decorous they look. When will Mrs. Walker tell everyone why she sent Amanda home? Amanda doesn't dare go back inside the hospital for her shawl and bonnet. Cassie can retrieve those tomorrow. She decides to walk through the alley, the way she used to go with Jed.

By now feeling steadier, she curses her every step. Jed went right back to his wife, nobody the wiser about Amanda's condition. After she opens her back gate, she hurls a stick at the bench hidden under the crape myrtles for good measure.

Chapter Seventeen

From the kitchen, Cassie hears the back gate clang. Missus emerges, bare head down, the front of her dress spattered. Her large feet clump up the path between the vegetable rows, splashing mud onto her skirt. The jerky motions of her arms and legs make her look like a chicken being chased.

Cassie puts down the spoon she is using to stir the potato soup and sighs. She moves the soup off the stove and covers the pot. Miss Nell settles down at the table to feed her doll some water and acorns, which she calls tea and cookies.

"Oh, Cassie," Missus says as she bursts through the back door, face red, rain slicking her broad cheeks. "I'm done for." She sobs, her muddy shoes slopping all over the clean floor.

"Mama, you're all wet!" says Nell.

Missus scowls.

"Sit down, now," says Cassie.

Missus shakes her head. "I'm going directly upstairs."

Cassie follows Missus as she climbs the stairs, huffing with outrage as well as effort. The hall leading the way to the bedroom is dim and Missus leans on the wall for support.

As Missus unbuttons her bodice, she says, "Mrs. Walker knows."

"You tell her?" says Cassie.

"Of course not! I fainted. When Betsy loosened my corset, Mrs. Walker saw."

Cassie pulls a clean dress from the wardrobe.

Amanda shakes her head. "No! Not that. I'll have to get into my wrapper now."

Cassie goes into the hall linen closet to get the wrapper, a loose-fitting dress with a flowing skirt meant for pregnant women. This angry side of Missus worries Cassie. What if she turns cruel and spiteful, like Miss Mildred? She hopes it's just a passing part of the pregnancy.

Miss Nell comes into the bedroom with her dolly, holding it close to her body as if it's a kitten.

Missus waves a hand and says, "Go away, Nell. Mama needs to rest."

The girl lowers her head and comes to Cassie, who puts an arm around her.

"I can't be seen anywhere in public now," says Missus.

"Take yourself to the garden. Can't nobody see in there," says Cassie.

"What's the use? Everything we planted will die next month."

"We need that food now, soldiers or no soldiers."

Cassie closes her eyes for a minute to try and think of how to calm Missus. When she opens them again, Missus is lying on her side, her knees pulled up towards her chest, the wrapper draped over the small arch of her belly. She breathes loudly but says nothing. Miss Nell has crept out of the room.

Cassie closes the window, shutting out the cool, rainy air. She busies herself laying a fire in the hearth. If Missus catches a cold, she will be in even more disagreeable spirits. Cassie kneels and sweeps the ashes of the previous fire aside, shaking them into a sack to take downstairs and save for making soft soap. After arranging the kindling in a triangle, she picks up the carrier to bring hot coals from the stove downstairs and light the fire for Missus.

"I'll eat supper in my room tonight," says Missus. "From now on, you will go to the market and the post office for me and take Nell with you. I will write a pass that you can use every day."

Cassie wants to shake Missus and tell her to let Miss Nell stay home, to pay attention to the daughter she already has instead of the baby she has to give away. She nods instead. These months before the baby comes will be a trial, but Cassie will be able to roam Richmond like never before. In church, she can listen more carefully to the whispered fragments about railroads and conductors, safe houses and friends. Running off by herself to an uncertain place up North holds little appeal, but Missus and her questions have ignited Cassie's longing for her family. Before now, Cassie always thought it was useless to do more than secretly pray for Clancy and the children. Yet things have changed because of Missus and her foolishness. Maybe with enough patience and quick wits, Cassie can at last find a chance to steal away and go back to her own people.

CHAPTER EIGHTEEN

Amanda begins most of her days feeling unsettled. When she wakes, it usually takes her a moment to remember where she is and why she can no longer leave the house. Some days, she expects to open her eyes and see the crisscrossed garlands of white flowers on the wallpaper in her bedroom at her aunt and uncle's house. Other times, she looks up into Mummy's eyes, the calm color of Virginia bluebells. Today, she remembers the heavy feel of Edwin's arm flung across her waist as he slept next to her.

Rolling onto her side, Amanda lifts Edwin's most recent letter from the bedside table. She keeps each letter here for a few days so she can read and reread it, parsing it for clues about when he might come home. After that, she stores the letters in the top right drawer of the bureau where she keeps her hair combs and jewelry. Jed's sketch is there too, buried under her handkerchiefs. Edwin's bureau drawer, where he left behind a comb, hair oil, and a jar of Mason's Blacking shoe polish, remains undisturbed.

> October 3, 1864
> My Dear Wife,
> Please forgive me for not writing to you sooner but we have had stirring times of late and have since been on the move to change camps. The Yankees appeared early one morning on the ridge above our camp just as we were dividing up our provisions. We formed our line right away. They surrounded us on three sides and we had to fall back through Winchester, and proceeded to press us so hard we had to travel nearly all night to stay ahead of them. There was a ghastly light in the sky from all the barns and mills that they burned as they went along. It makes me sick at heart to see this kind of wanton destruction.
> We are still moving south, marching and fighting along

the way. One day, it rained so much, I felt wet as a drowned rat despite my oilcloth. Some men took off their ill-fitting shoes and carried them so as to give their sore feet some relief. We are still on the move, so I will send more news as I am able. I have heard that we will make a winter camp soon. It will be good to rest after being jarred around so much.

Right now, as the mornings start out frosty, home and all its comforts seem like a distant dream. How I long to see you and our dear Nell, but I must continue serving. I must wait patiently for the time to come when I will be able to return to you. When it does, may I make you happy and in so doing feel happy in return.

Now I end this letter in haste, as soon we will pass Harrisonburg and I will have the opportunity to mail it there.

Your loving husband,
Edwin

Amanda refolds the letter and puts it back on the table. He likely omits the worst details, never mentioning feeling frightened or heartsick at seeing so many dead and wounded comrades. To admit any kind of despondence would make him seem unpatriotic. Yet she is grateful that he remains safe, and especially that this letter gives her no reason to worry about his imminent return.

Cassie knocks softly at the door. When Amanda tells her to come in, Cassie brings in a breakfast tray. An envelope rests next to the teacup and saucer. She is surprised that Edwin is writing so soon after his last letter. But when she looks more closely at the envelope, she sees handwriting in larger and messier letters than Edwin would ever form. She can make out the return address from North Carolina.

"Go see to Nell now," she orders Cassie.

Cassie nods and picks up Amanda's chamber pot to empty

it into the privy.

Alone again, Amanda pushes the bedclothes back so fast that they fall to the floor. She rips open the envelope.

> *October 11, 1864*
> *Dear Mrs. Carter,*
>
> *As you can see from this letter, I am home now and getting along as best I can. I found work repairing wagon wheels and such. My boys help me with chores.*
>
> *I have thought much on what to do about the delivery you are expecting this winter. Well, I wasn't going to tell no one of it but Annie, my older sister, she asked me all about my time in Richmond and now she knows. She offers to take your package if you will deliver it to her. She is a good woman with three daughters. Her husband is gone to fight near Wilmington but her father-in-law lives with her and works on the place. I look in on them so I can see to their well-being.*
>
> *If you agree with this plan write to Mrs. A. A. Spencer, Washington, North Carolina. So I will close for this time with the hope that you are in good health.*
> *Jed Griffin*

Beneath his signature, he has drawn a picture of a wooden home with a front porch running its entire width. A door stands in the middle between two windows. Four white columns hold up a steeply sloped roof. A hound with a sleek, dark coat sleeps under the chair, head on his paws, a whip of a tail stretched behind him. "Annie's house," he has written underneath.

Amanda traces each of Jed's sentences with her forefinger. She knows he has to be careful about what he says in case his wife or Edwin come across the letter. Still, she wants more from him—words like "affectionately," "devotedly," or even "true loving." She wants to stand at the bottom of the porch rail, holding his hand, free to go inside with him. What if she could be his wife, lively and graceful next to him?

She dangles her long legs off the bed and then stands up. Her growing girth makes every movement awkward. When she pushes aside the curtains, she sees tomato leaves, their edges browned and shriveled from frost. What would it really be like to live with a man who could not push a plow or even walk up the front porch stairs without assistance? Would Jed's charms wear thin as he relied on her to do basic tasks, such as bringing in firewood? He had no money for slaves to help him. His wife probably worked so much she had no time to plant flowers with her red and callused hands.

Jed didn't include a sketch of his sister, but Amanda pictures a woman with a broad back and upper arms thick as loaves of bread. She must be kind to offer to add to her household at such a time, especially when her husband is in peril. Will she still want the baby if it is a girl?

Amanda folds the letter and holds it against her cheek. Her swollen belly feels like a dome that covers not only the baby but also her bed, the entire house, and even the miles between Richmond and Washington, North Carolina. How would she make her way to such a place? The only time she traveled was during the move to Richmond after she married Edwin. Yet the trip to North Carolina will take her far from the mockery she has made of the Carter name. She will come back unburdened, ready to receive Edwin the way a proper wife should.

She climbs back into bed, ready to carefully compose the letter at her lap desk. It must sound impersonal in case Jed's wife or someone else sees it and learns what she is really trying to communicate.

October 19, 1864
Dear Mrs. Spencer,
Private Jed Griffin, whom I met in Richmond, has written me a letter of introduction to you. I greatly appreci-

ate your kindness at this time.

I will be much obliged to accept your generous offer. I expect my package to be ready in late January or early February. I will send word of when I might be able to deliver it to you. For now, I extend to you my deepest gratitude and kindest regards.

Yours very truly,
Mrs. Amanda Carter

Before she has time to rethink her decision, she scrawls Mrs. Spencer's name and address across the front and calls Cassie to come and take her letter to the post office.

CHAPTER NINETEEN

Cassie comes into the parlor with a dust rag and sees that Missus glows like a gas lamp burns within her. Missus looks up from the scarf she knits for Master Carter. Bits of straw poke out from the wool, and the mulberry dye didn't take well, but it's the only yarn Cassie can find in the shops. Missus wants to finish it in time to send it to him for Christmas. This is the only kind of knitting she seems able to do—one row after the other, no stopping and starting for fancy patterns.

"Oh, Cassie, good news," says Missus.

"What do Master Carter say?"

"That letter wasn't from Master Carter."

"Who then? Your aunt want to see you after all?"

"No. It was from Private Griffin."

"That soldier? He still sweet-talking you?"

"It's not like that. The most wonderful thing happened. His sister wants to take the baby!" Her voice crescendos to a high pitch, making her sound as young and excitable as Miss Nell.

Cassie sets down her rag and faces Missus. "That so?"

"After the baby is born, you, Nell and I will go down to North Carolina to take him there."

Cassie's hand trembles, and she leans against the end table to steady herself. The air in the parlor feels heavy, like a sultry afternoon right before the first crack of thunder. She tastes something metallic in her mouth, swallows, and carefully weighs her words. This could be her chance, finally, to leave Richmond—but she has to play it carefully. What she wants is to take the baby to North Carolina on her own, without Missus Carter or Miss Nell, and never come back.

"What happen if Master Carter come home while we gone?"

Amanda frowns. "Oh, I don't know. We can leave word

that I went to visit my aunt and uncle."

"Your aunt always vex you. He know that."

"True, but maybe I can say it's safer out at her place than here in Richmond."

"And when he come out there looking for you?"

Missus's needles click and keep clicking.

"Oh, Cassie, I don't know!" she finally says. "I'll just have to take my chances. I'd rather the baby go to a good home near his father than to the Sisters of Charity."

Cassie picks up the clock on the mantel, runs the rag under it, and walks into the kitchen. Each step threatens to betray her shaking legs. She pours herself a glass of water and sags onto her stool. Even though she has never ridden a train, she wants to climb aboard a car that speeds across the wide, muddy James River past the jumble of buildings in Manchester on the bank opposite Richmond. The wriggling baby in her arms will be just a temporary encumbrance before she goes to Julia and Gabriel. But how can she convince Missus to let her go?

Nell pads into the kitchen, cheeks pink, one side of her hair pushed up from lying down while napping. She climbs into Cassie's lap and rests a cheek against her chest. Cassie clamps her mouth shut and strokes the girl's back. What will become of Nell? This is not the right moment to speak up. That moment might only come once, so Cassie needs to prepare herself.

CHAPTER TWENTY

Amanda spends more and more time on the couch, a quilt wrapped around her legs. Its winding blades pattern has a white X in the middle and blue V shapes inside each square. Aunt Margaret gave it to her as a wedding gift. The careful workmanship mocks Amanda's sprawling belly. Her view has shrunk to the quadrant of East Grace Street that she can see from her front windows.

Now that she is no longer struggling to decide what to do about the baby, she has more patience for Nell. Her lap has become too big to accommodate the girl, but Nell is grateful for the time with her mother and wants to be good, so she follows Amanda's instructions not to talk about her mother's growing belly. She has started snuggling at her side while Amanda reads aloud poems by Henry Wadsworth Longfellow. Amanda knows she should not be glorifying a man from the enemy territory of Massachusetts, but her own mother used to sit beside Amanda's bed and recite his poems in her gentle English accent. Amanda finds Longfellow's words stirring and Nell likes to follow along. "*I heard the trailing garments of the Night / Sweep through her marble halls....*"

After Nell gets up, the wallpaper in the parlor feels as though it is pressing against Amanda's temples. When Cassie comes in with the *Daily Dispatch*, Amanda says, "I'm glad to look at something besides that dreary wall."

"You ain't used to staying home."

Amanda shrugs and looks down at the headlines. The "War News" column carries little new information these days. Confederate troops, dug into their winter quarters at Petersburg, march through Richmond less frequently. The blockade and damage to the railroads have kept freshly wounded soldiers and refugees from other parts of the Confederacy to a minimum, too.

Despite the lull in fighting, the entire Confederate military force has become diminished and ill supplied. The situation is so dire that the Confederate legislature has voted to send a peace delegation to Washington. As much as Amanda wants the privations of life in Richmond and the loss of so many lives to end with a peace treaty, she also wants Edwin's homecoming delayed as long as possible.

"As soon as this war ends and the shops fill up with goods again," she says to Cassie, "I want to put something lighter and more modern on the walls. Maybe a pattern with flowers painted on it. Mildred must have been some kind of gloomy."

"Don't trouble yourself about the first Missus Carter."

"Was she pretty?"

"You the one here now."

Even now, Amanda can feel the imprints of Mildred's fragile body everywhere—in the bed, on the sofa, in the dining chairs. The first Mrs. Carter never had to watch Edwin enlist, never had to hold a cup of water for a wounded man or write a letter home to the man's sweetheart, someone dear he might never see again. Edwin never left that Mrs. Carter home alone for months on end after he married her. She stayed by his side, the dutiful and virtuous wife, ready to reward him with a child until the birth went so terribly wrong. Amanda can never measure up to her.

Telling Cassie she needs fresh air, Amanda pushes herself upright, slips on her cloak, and goes out into the garden to cut holly sprigs. The ground crunches under her black leather boots with side laces. The dormant garden looks as drab as the fraying hem of her faded, teal-colored wrapper. She pokes the ice in the cistern with a stick and wonders what might have happened had she convinced Edwin to stay home from the war. Edwin's brother had simply paid someone to go in his place. His brother had also refused to let Edwin take one of the farm's horses. Edwin was forced to join the infantry instead of the cavalry, where he might have been spared the drudgery and discomfort of so many footsore marches.

A week before Edwin was due to leave with his company, Amanda stayed in bed as Edwin closed the door, set down his washbasin in front of the mirror, and took out his razor and a towel. They had gone to bed at the same time the night before, their skin glued together by the July humidity. When she kissed him, she felt like she was drinking him in, as if that could fortify her against the fear of watching him leave and never return. The bed was a raft, a safe place in the constant swirl of soldiers throughout the city.

In the first months of their marriage, Amanda felt like she was mostly lying back, letting him have his way in bed. When she became pregnant, he was so afraid of harming the baby that he stopped marital relations altogether. Only after Nell's birth, when he came back to her tentatively, gently, did she learn to move along with him.

Amanda watched as Edwin soaped his chin, then contorted his face to help the razor glide smoothly. In his dark purple dressing gown, his white cheeks made him look ghostly.

"Nothing like a good shave," he said.

"Nothing I'd know about," she retorted.

"No, I wouldn't expect so," he said. Then he wiped his face and turned to her. In two strides, he lifted the covers and slid in. He pulled one of her curls until it looked like a straight lock of hair, then let go so that it sprang into loops again. His smooth face still smelled of soap. Up close, she could see a spot he missed and rubbed her fingertip across it until it rasped. As his hand meandered over her breasts, she closed her eyes. She wasn't used to such intimacy in daylight. She wondered if his ardor would leave her with a new child to be born in his absence. Amanda wanted more children, but not until Edwin returned from the war. It would be folly to raise a large family without a husband.

After they had joined together, Edwin rolled to the other side of the bed and sat up. She reached out and touched his waist. After he left, she and Nell would have no family in Richmond, no ties to the city at all. Nell had turned one year old in May of 1861. Amanda could imagine her own footsteps thumping through empty rooms, the way they had after her parents died.

"Do you really have to leave? You have a good business. Doesn't your tobacco help the war by keeping up the morale of the soldiers?"

"There's no honor in that."

"I'll be left alone with nothing but honor."

He sighed. "How's my gray jacket coming along?"

"That's up to Cassie. You know I have no head for sewing."

"You have no head for the cause, either, it seems."

"I do, but Nell and I will be stuck alone in this dangerous city, choked off from everything. What if you...if you..." She couldn't bear to finish the sentence about his not coming back, but he seemed to understand.

He stood up. "I have a duty. You seem to have forgotten yours as a Southern citizen."

He paused in buttoning his pants and looked back at her.

"A little sacrifice, Mrs. Carter. A few months and we'll push those Yankees back north to Washington City and be done with them. I'll come home, we'll have more children, and we'll raise our family in the only country I'm proud of, the Confederate States of America."

Amanda stood up and rearranged the bedcovers. "What will I do here?"

"Look after Nell and find some ladies who are making bandages or mending uniforms or doing other things to help out," he said.

Then he poured water over his hands, wiped them, and walked out, shutting the door behind him.

Now Amanda shivers as she fills a bucket of water for the

holly, then returns to the house. In the kitchen, Cassie prepares a special Christmas dessert from four precious eggs, their last half-cup of sugar, and a few spoonsful of flour. She has also set aside two oranges that Lizzie gave her after church on Sunday. When Amanda comes in, Cassie takes the holly sprigs and begins to tie them together into a garland for the mantel. Nell crawls on the floor to pick up the berries that have fallen.

"Can we eat these, Mama?" she asks.

"Oh, no, they'll make you sick," says Amanda, holding out her hand for Nell to give her the berries.

A knock at the front door startles them. Amanda straightens, panic squeezing her throat. The knock comes again. What if Edwin has come home to surprise her for Christmas? In his last letter, he wrote that he was trying to stay warm in a hut near Staunton, Virginia, with five other men, one of whom coughed all night. Maybe he has taken ill again and the army sent him home to recover.

She rushes upstairs, arriving out of breath. The baby jabs her bladder with a kick as she closes her bedroom door and tries to decide what to do if Edwin has indeed arrived. Could she get under the covers and feign a terrible fever?

The front door creaks open and Cassie says to the caller, "Good evening, ma'am."

Amanda's back sags with relief. She feels almost giddy.

"Merry Christmas," she hears in the familiar, ringing tones of Mrs. Walker. "How is Mrs. Carter getting along?"

"Oh, fine," says Cassie. "Merry Christmas to you, Missus Walker."

"Well, I'm sure she's resting, but I'm leaving this basket. See that she gets this note, too."

"I surely will. Thank you, ma'am," says Cassie and shuts the door. Then she comes upstairs and knocks. Amanda calls to her to open the door, and Nell follows her in.

"Mama, your face is all red," says Nell.

In the basket, wrapped in a linen cloth, Amanda finds a dozen raisin-studded yeast buns, still warm, and a Bible along with a note.

> *Dear Mrs. Carter,*
> *I have prayed for you. The Lord Jesus shows infinite mercy and forgiveness to you and all of God's children. Please accept this Bible and as my gift. I will call on you again. Merry Christmas.*
> *May peace be with you,*
> *Mrs. Caroline Walker*

"Well!" says Amanda, tears in her eyes, then begins to sing a Christmas carol that her mother taught her. "*Peace on earth and mercy mild.*"

Nell reaches for a raisin bun.

"*God and sinners reconciled,*" sings Cassie, picking up the next line.

Chapter Twenty-one

Amanda scans Edwin's new letter and wonders how he can still sound so fervent about the Confederacy. Food shortages are bad enough in Richmond that the city set up a soup house in the basement of Metropolitan Hall. The city of Petersburg seems a shambles. Any homes near the front have been taken over or torn down for firewood, the outhouses the first to go. General Sherman left Atlanta and overran Savannah in December, destroying the railroads and cutting the telegraph lines. Reports indicate that he is now heading into South Carolina. Amanda wonders if the general will keep marching straight to Richmond, burning and pillaging as he goes. How would it feel to watch lines of uniformed enemies snaking along Broad Street? To be a civilian ordered around at gunpoint?

Out in the field, Edwin doesn't have to be terrified about having his city overtaken and his possessions pillaged and burned. He is hunkered down, waiting the thaw that will bring fresh battles.

> *January 5, 1865*
> *My Dear Wife,*
>
> *I take a few minutes to write to you and thank you for the scarf that you knitted for me. Your kindness keeps me warm and comfortably clad. The wind cannot be kept out of these huts, no matter how many rags we stuff into the cracks, so I have taken to wearing the scarf night and day.*
>
> *You ask if I lose heart after the months and years of battles that have kept me so far away from you and our dear little one. It is not for ourselves alone that we labor. To end this war now would allow the Yankees to subjugate us, to cause us to lose all freedom of thought and speech. There is no honor in surrender. No, not when our Southern nationhood is at stake.*

As you know, our motto as Virginians is "sic semper tyr-
annis"—we will not submit to tyrants. I'm afraid there will
be more suffering and bloodshed, but we must make sure that
the war ceases on honorable terms. We must continue to press
ahead or all that we have fought for will be lost.

Kiss Nell for me and keep up your courage. I am doing
all that I can.

With every affection,
Edwin

Amanda uses her elbows to push her heavy body up from the parlor sofa, folds the letter, and places it in a basket in the entry hall to bring upstairs. Peering out the front window to the sleet-spattered street, Amanda sees Mrs. Walker in a gray cloak, head bent against the wind. She carefully opens the gate and comes up the stairs. Clothed in a wrapper and wool socks, Amanda makes her way upstairs, straining for breath by the time she reaches the top. She is not presentable like this.

Downstairs, Cassie greets Mrs. Walker and offers to hang her wet wrap near the kitchen stove. Then she comes up to tell Amanda that Mrs. Walker wants to see her.

"Like this?" says Amanda gesturing to her stomach.

"She ask for you."

"What am I going to do?"

Cassie pours half a pitcher of water into the washbasin and dips a comb in it. In the looking glass, Amanda sees a smudge of black curls around a face swollen with eight months of pregnancy. Cassie works through Amanda's hair with the wet comb, wraps the mass into a bun, and pushes five hairpins into it. Then she pulls a paisley shawl out of the drawer and motions for Amanda to wrap it around her shoulders.

When Amanda comes into the parlor, Mrs. Walker is settled on the sofa, patting the lace on the collar of her claret-colored wool dress into place. Amanda clumsily lowers herself into the armchair, her backside landing with a thud, and pulls the quilt over her lap. Why does Mrs. Walker bother to dress like a fine lady when she is visiting a fallen woman? Can't she leave well enough alone?

"This weather surely tests our faith and perseverance," says Mrs. Walker, her cheeks red from the cold. Drops of sleet line the tendrils of hair at her temples, making it look like her face is surrounded by jewels. She arranges her skirt around her, taking up most of the sofa, and puts a bag of knitting on the floor beside her feet.

"Have you been reading the Bible I sent over?" she asks.

"Some. And thank you kindly for sending it."

Amanda has tried to mark passages that capture her attention, but so far she finds the words as slippery as the wet cobblestones outside.

"Keep reading. Jesus said, '*I am the light of the world: he that followeth me shall not walk in darkness, but shall have the light of life*,'" says Mrs. Walker, pulling out a ball of yarn, needles, and a half-finished sock.

Amanda rearranges the quilt across her lap. She traces the tidy stitching and wonders whether Mrs. Walker has come to lead her own private Bible class. Cassie brings two cups of hot water flavored with dried apples and leaves the room.

Mrs. Walker says, her voice trembling, "Mrs. Carter, I have been praying for you.

Amanda flattens her palms against the chair arms. She never brings her hands together to pray. If she closes her eyes and tries to talk to Jesus, it feels like her words roar away in a gust of wind.

"Thank you," she forces herself to say.

Mrs. Walker pulls out a handkerchief and wipes her eyes before continuing. "My older sister was once in your condition. Her sweetheart jilted her and moved back up to the mountains where he came from. When our mother and father found out, they sent her away to a family in Philadelphia who would take her on as a maid. I have never heard from her or seen her again."

Amanda shudders. She's lucky to be able to stay home, though she has to hide indoors. "I'm sorry about that," she says.

"Reverend Walker does not know that I have come to see you. But for my sister's sake, I want to help you. I think we could find a family who would take your baby. When the time comes, I would just tell him that I heard of a baby that needs a home—he need not know whose baby it is. He could ask in his congregation."

Amanda imagines Mrs. Walker wrapping the baby in her cloak and carrying it down the street into her home, where so many soldiers have suffered. Then a strange woman would come into her parlor and take the baby somewhere in the labyrinth of Richmond's streets. The idea horrifies her. Every time she goes out, she will search the face of every child, wondering if it belongs to her. It's better to send the baby far away so she has no reminder of what she did wrong.

"But I already made arrangements," Amanda says.

Mrs. Walker looks up, a crease between her brows. "Have you sent word to the Sisters?"

"No. The father's sister is willing to take the baby. She lives near him in North Carolina. He said he can keep an eye on things."

"But what of the child's religious education? Surely you want to raise a God-fearing child, not a heathen. A family from the church will provide for that."

"The baby's aunt will provide a good home."

"How will you bring a newborn on such a trip?"

"I'll go with my servant, Cassie. I have no brothers, and no father in this world to escort me."

Cassie returns to pick up the empty cups. Mrs. Walker frowns and rubs a length of yarn between her forefinger and thumb. Then she leans closer to Amanda and confides, "The wartime trains and roads are no place for a new mother and her children. I've heard talk about those soldiers out on picket. The Lord knows what the Yankees might do. Our boys, too. They have to behave well when they are in my home. But when they go off into their camps, they can be a rough lot. They have no respect for a lady."

"I'm not very respectable anymore."

"You need not go asking for more trouble."

"But I've chosen the home that I want for my baby."

"You still have some time before your confinement. I ask you to consider what a good, Christian family here in Richmond could offer."

Mrs. Walker lays her knitting in her lap and picks up the Bible. "I want to read you something," she says. "It's from John 8:11. *Jesus said to the adulteress, 'Neither do I condemn thee: go and sin no more.'*"

"Oh, I am done with sin," says Amanda. "Now and forever am I done with sin."

"Then you must pray for His mercy."

Amanda closes her eyes and hears the wind rush. The Bible verse tells her to go, and that's what she plans to do, no matter how much Mrs. Walker urges her to reconsider.

Chapter Twenty-two

After church on the first Sunday in January, Cassie follows Lizzie to her home, walking briskly. The bright, cold air stings her cheeks, reinvigorating her after the preacher's somnolent sermon about how running to the Yankee enemy is a sin, and "all sin is contrary to the law of God." Lumps of dirt in the street have frozen into place today, making her footing precarious in the worn boots that Missus handed down to her. Cassie stuffed the toes with rags but they still slide around on her small feet.

Cassie rubs her hands together, trying to warm them up. At the pine table in her back room, Lizzie pours a thin layer of dirt in a baking pan and leans over it.

"Ready for your learning?"

Cassie smiles.

Lizzie traces letters of the alphabet with a stick while Cassie sounds out each one: "Buh-buh-buh." "You-you-you."

"Now, put them together with a lah, lah, lah in the middle," Lizzie says, spelling out the word B-L-U-E.

"Buh-buh-buh-lah-oooh!" Cassie sings out. "Blue. Blue! I read them letters. Praise the Lord!"

They both laugh.

"You learning, but shh," says Lizzie, pointing to the ceiling. A cook and his family live upstairs. They have to keep these lessons secret. Anyone caught teaching a slave to read, including a free Negro like Lizzie, risks being flogged and fined. If Lizzie can't pay the fine, she also risks being sold back into slavery.

"Blue, blue, blue," whispers Cassie, looking up, her mouth turned up like the letter U.

Lizzie pulls a Bible from behind a rack of dried rosemary. Cassie's goal to be able to read from it still seems far off, yet Lizzie promised to teach her the first sentence in John 1:1 before Missus Carter's baby is born: "*In the beginning was the Word, and the Word was with God, and the Word was God.*" They get through "in" and "the" before Cassie stumbles on the "g" in "beginning."

"All them letters bunched up together," says Cassie, pointing with her finger at the page. "Little specks of letters."

"You need more time," says Lizzie.

"All I got is time right now. Too much. Waiting, waiting, waiting," says Cassie.

"You best make the most of it."

"How? I look outside, I see her garden. Her walls. Inside, her baby on the way."

Lizzie brushes the dirt in the pan until it's blank again. "Always that way with white folks. Their homes, their rules, their sins we got to mop up after. Only way I get free is when my master decide to make me free when he die."

"White folks decide everything."

"She treat you bad?"

"No, but she can't do nothing for herself. Nothing for her daughter, neither. I worry about that girl."

"You leaving soon enough."

"Maybe not."

"She change her mind?"

"The preacher lady's wife come over and tell her to leave the baby with a family in Richmond."

"Look for a way to go without her, then. Lots of folks running now, even in winter. Contraband camps everywhere you find Yankee camps."

"Cont-tra—what?"

"Contraband. That's what they call slave folks who run to the Yankees. Anyone who get behind the lines can stay put. You know how the preacher talk today, running to the Yankees a sin? He warning us."

"That so? What if I go to them Yankees but get myself killed first or sold south and never get back to my young'uns?"

"The Lord has a plan for you, for me, for everyone."

"Well, I'm mighty tired of waiting to find out what His plan is for me."

"No sense in trying to know the mystery. No one can."

Cassie runs her fingers across the open page of the Bible and closes her eyes. Why can't the words of comfort that surely must be printed there soak into her hand like a salve?

"Pray for patience," says Lizzie.

"You best make me one of them tonics for patience. That the only way this body going to get any," says Cassie.

CHAPTER TWENTY-THREE

Nell comes into the parlor to show Amanda the new costume she made for her doll. The store-bought, cloth lady doll stands about eighteen inches high, with a china head and dark brown, painted-on hair. Nell named her Rose. Today, Nell has tucked rags underneath the doll's dress to imitate Amanda's girth.

Amanda frowns. "Don't make her look like that. It's not suitable."

"But she looks like you. Shh! She's resting," Nells says as she leans over the sofa and slides the doll underneath the quilt in Amanda's lap.

Amanda smiles weakly, too tired to protest. The girl's long fingers delicately taper, giving her an advantage for needlework or piano playing. Her body is growing so fast, her knees are beginning to show under her hem. Cassie will need to cut down one of Amanda's old dresses or add a strip of fabric to the bottom of this one to get her through another season. At this rate, she will one day be as tall as Amanda. Once Amanda can leave the house again, she plans to take Nell to pick out pretty fabric for a new dress—maybe even something imported from England, if that's possible anymore. Her daughter should have clothes that fit properly.

The back door opens and Nell leaves her mother to see what Cassie is doing in the kitchen. Amanda hears the murmur of their voices and the light scrape of Cassie rearranging the flour and meal bins on the pantry shelf.

Soon, Cassie comes into the parlor with a log for the fire.

"I can't get comfortable today," says Amanda, squirming and adjusting the pillow behind her. "I hope it won't be long now."

"Every baby come in its own time."

"Is Lizzie ready to come when we need her?" Amanda asks.

When Nell was born, Edwin sent for a doctor. He wouldn't take any chances with a midwife after what happened to Mildred. Of course, that was not possible now.

"Yes, ma'am."

"When do you think I'll be able to travel?"

"Depend on how you feel after the baby come out."

"Are you ready for the trip?"

Cassie is silent for so long that Amanda wonders if she heard the question. The fire throws orange shadows against her face, making it look outsized, while her dress seems to swallow her small body.

Cassie puts down the log, leaving the top of her headscarf instead of her face visible to Amanda. When she looks up again, she speaks slowly, eyes on the floor.

"I be ready when you tell me. But maybe if…"

"If what?"

"If you ain't of a mind to travel, you and Miss Nell…you stay home. I take the baby."

"But I can't just send you out there on your own. How would you know where to go?" Amanda pictures Cassie lost in a thicket, brambles catching at her dress and at the blanket of the precious baby she holds in her arms, with no one trustworthy to ask for help.

"You tell me the name of the place, you write that on the pass."

"I don't know."

"Master Carter come back, you and Miss Nell still be here. Everything the same for him," says Cassie.

"But what about you?" says Amanda, heaving herself to her feet and pacing around the room. Every day, she reads the ads in the *Dispatch* offering rewards for the return of escaped Negroes of all types—men, women, gingerbread color, jet black, stout, short, bushy-haired, lame. What if Cassie simply runs off with the baby?

"No trouble for me to take care of a baby anyplace," says Cassie, then turns to go back into the kitchen.

Amanda watches Cassie's steady footing and straight back. Placing one hand on each side of her stomach, she circles from sofa to fireplace a few more times, trying to make up her mind. Is it too much to risk? What if either one falls ill on the journey? What if a bandit robs Cassie and leaves her with no means to keep traveling? Worse, a gang of slave hunters could capture Cassie. Profiteers are always ready to sell a Negro woman, even if she isn't for sale. There's no telling where the baby would end up if something like that happened. Still, the sooner Cassie takes the baby away, the sooner Amanda will have nothing to hide.

CHAPTER TWENTY-FOUR

Amanda's labor begins before first light on a blustery morning, when the gush of her water breaking wakes her.

"Cassie?" she calls, but no one answers. Branches of the magnolia scrape the side of the house.

Amanda stuffs a towel inside her underdrawers and slowly makes her way down to Cassie's room behind the pantry. With her knuckle, she taps at the closed door.

Cassie comes out, her hair sticking up in tufts, a blanket wrapped around her.

"It's time," says Amanda.

Cassie blinks and nods. "I get Lizzie," she says, and turns to walk back into her room.

Amanda panics and clutches Cassie's arm. "Don't leave me alone."

"Your pains start yet?"

"No."

"Best get back to bed. Baby not coming for awhile."

"What if Nell wakes up?"

"Tell her you resting. I be back before full sunup."

Cassie lets the blanket slide off her. She wears one of Amanda's cast-off chemises, which is so long on her that it grazes the floor. One bare shoulder pokes out of it. She shivers as she helps Amanda upstairs.

"It still dark out. Need me a special pass to go out and find Lizzie," Cassie says.

Amanda sighs in exasperation. "Oh, what a bother! Bring me a pen and a sheet of Master Carter's stationery. Hurry up!"

Under the Carter Tobacco name and address, Amanda scrawls

January 16, 1865
Please let my servant, Cassie, travel to the home of Liz-
zie, a free woman of color who lives near the First African
Baptist Church in Richmond, and back this morning
Mrs. Carter

The first contraction seizes Amanda before Cassie returns. She clutches a wad of the top bedsheet in each hand, willing herself not to cry out and wake Nell. There will be no authoritative doctor to help her through this delivery. Even after the contraction passes, fear keeps her body rigid—fear of pain from the next contraction, fear of losing the baby after all the waiting and worry, fear of losing her own life and leaving Nell without a mother and Edwin widowed for no reason but her own imprudence.

Lizzie arrives to help Amanda ride out the successive bursts of pain that rack her, giving her sips of lukewarm raspberry leaf tea in between. Cassie looks after Nell.

At nightfall, Amanda gives one final push and out slides the baby.

"Missus Carter, you have yourself a boy," says Lizzie.

Amanda is too overwhelmed to speak.

Lizzie washes the tiny body with a rag dipped in warm water and wraps him in a clean towel. Cassie comes in with an extra candle so Amanda can see his face. Even in the flickering light, she can tell that his reddish fuzz of hair and the extra-long space between his upper lip and his nose look unmistakably like Jed.

Cassie puts the baby on Amanda's chest. His breath softly flutters one of her curls. She strokes his back and lets his damp weight pin her to the pillow.

"Jacob," she whispers, the first syllable an exhalation and then the "b" pulling her lips closed. The "J" comes from Jed; otherwise, she simply likes the name. "Jacob, Jacob, Jacob," she repeats, as if the incantation could cast a spell against her having to send him away.

CHAPTER TWENTY-FIVE

Amanda keeps Jacob's cradle next to her bed. Sometimes, when she wakes up in the night and cannot hear his breathing, she holds a finger under his nose. She wants to feel the breeze of his tiny presence. When she goes back to bed, she pulls the covers over her head, trying to banish the restless shadow of Mildred giving birth in this same bed.

She tells Nell that the baby is theirs to play with but not to keep.

"He belongs to another family," she says when Nell asks why he can't stay with them.

Nell likes to pat his head or lay an arm against his back when the three of them sit on the couch with the book of Longfellow poems. But she gets frustrated, too.

When he cries, she says, "Leave him there."

"He's hungry! We take care of you when you're hungry," says Amanda.

"I'm hungry, too."

"Go ask Cassie to give you some soup."

Today, Amanda nurses Jacob, then brings him downstairs. She wraps him in a triple layer of blankets and carries him into the garden. Bright sun takes the sting out of the cold air. She circles the dormant vegetable patch and Lenten rose bushes, Jacob anchoring her. Cassie comes out with a basket of clean laundry. Her red headscarf bobs as she stoops to pick up a diaper and reaches up to pin it to the line.

By the end of February, they will have to make their way south. Amanda dreads the trip. Her bottom still feels raw, and her breasts leak milk every time Jacob cries. She thought her energy would come right back, as it had with Nell, but she still feels stout and unbalanced. This cloistered garden protects her, yet she knows that every day she waits to leave, the possibility of

Edwin coming home grows stronger. His brigade still suffers through the harsh winter in their encampment near Winchester, but he writes that they are likely to confront the enemy again as soon as the weather breaks.

Can Cassie be trusted to take Jacob to North Carolina on her own? She has always done her work without loafing around or sassing, always taken good care of Nell. She goes out in Richmond to do the household errands and always returns. Sending her to North Carolina might be the best chance Amanda will have to fully recover from childbirth and be ready for Edwin no matter when he comes home. Edwin would never know anything went wrong while he was away. If he came home when Cassie was traveling, Amanda would say that Cassie ran away. Convincing Nell to keep the baby a secret might prove more difficult, but she would think of something to tell the girl.

Cassie finishes hanging the laundry and asks what to make for dinner.

"Minute pudding, I suppose."

"Low on milk, but can mix in water."

Amanda looks down at Jacob. He blinks at the magnolia branches above him. "I wish he didn't have to leave," she says.

"How you going to hide a baby you ain't supposed to have?"

"I know. I just...I can't bear to think of him so far away when I..." her voice falters.

From between two baby blankets on the clothesline, Cassie looks steadily at Amanda, waiting for her to continue.

"Oh, Cassie, how can I possibly give my baby to anyone else?" says Amanda.

The empty sack of clothespins droops in Cassie's hand. "It ain't natural but sometimes that's the way it's got to be," she snaps.

Amanda instantly feels flustered and foolish. What has she said? Cassie, too, was forced to give up her children. Amanda puts the back of one hand in front of her mouth and cradles Jacob with the other. Maybe she won't have to do what seems impossible if Cassie does it for her. When Cassie returns, Amanda wants to arrange for her to see her own children—maybe even by setting her free, no matter how much Edwin might protest.

"Yes, you're right," Amanda says quietly. "And I have decided it would be easier for me if you bring Jacob to his new family on your own. You said you were willing to travel with him. Now I've made up my mind. I'd like you to go."

"Yes'm," says Cassie, not turning away fast enough to hide her tear-slicked cheeks from Amanda.

CHAPTER TWENTY-SIX

Holding a candle, Cassie kneels before the family shrine in her room and thanks Jesus for rewarding her with the patience Lizzie urged her to find. Many times before today, Cassie wanted to ask Missus what she decided about taking Jacob to North Carolina, but she had to keep her tongue stiff as a clapper in a bell. Now she has received her reward.

Cassie rearranges Gabriel's shriveled chestnuts and green cloth next to Julia's rag doll, then sniffs the piece of horse halter to see if it still smells like Clancy. It does, but faintly. Will he still be there when she returns, or will Master Scruggs have sold him? With his skills as a horseman, he would bring a high price. What about Julia? She must be grown by now. Will she still remember her mama? Gabriel, barely able to walk when she left, will probably think she's a stranger. Either one—or both —could have been sold, too, especially if Master Scruggs kept up his gambling.

She surveys the room where she has spent more than ten years. What is there to take? A winter dress, a summer dress, a cloak, a few head scarves, the boots Missus handed down, needles and thread, maybe a blanket. Her most precious possession, her daughter's hair ribbon, can easily fit in the bottom of a satchel.

When she blows out the candle and closes her eyes, she remains awake. Since she first spread the blankets that Miss Mildred gave her onto the pallet in this room, she has plotted her escape. She always thought she would have to go furtively at night, hoping that whispered conversations and reliable people would lead her back to Clancy and her children at the Scruggs place. Now she will have a real pass from Missus, a white person's permission to travel. As soon as she drops off the baby, she can make her way back to Dinwiddie County, where the Scruggs family lives. Once she finds her children, she isn't sure what to do next. Staying nearby without Master Scruggs or one of his sons discovering her would be risky. Sneaking across Union lines would keep her from having to return to the Carters, but would her children be able to run away with her, avoiding the slave patrols that Master Scruggs would surely send out?

Cassie will be glad to leave Richmond. Missus Carter's more frequent errands in the past months have given her more of a chance to get off Church Hill and learn the ways of the vendors at First Market and in the business district. But as a colored woman, she never can walk beneath the shade trees or on the grassy fringe of Capitol Square unless she accompanies a white person. The constant traffic in the streets, especially the drills and parades of soldiers, exhaust her. At the Scruggs place, there was comfort at night in the sound of crickets and raccoon calls instead of horses, drums, and marching boots. All she wants is a quiet place to live and take care of herself and her children.

Miss Nell will suffer most after she leaves. The girl counts on her from the minute she wakes up hungry for breakfast. Missus still doesn't act like she's in charge of her own daughter. Maybe giving up the baby will help her do more for Miss Nell. What Missus really needs to do is pay attention. The girl generally asks for everything she needs.

When Cassie finally falls asleep, she dreams that she skirts the upper field at the Scruggs place, where the last rows of tobacco grow raggedy. A trail through the thick pines begins at the end of the third row. She covers the ground quickly in her bare feet, softly clapping and pointing the way to Julia so she won't have to talk. Gabriel rides her hip, his arms circling her torso. It's damp and cool in the woods. The pine needles carpet the trail, protecting their feet from sharp rocks. Over the rise, she spots the gush and sparkle of the river. Clancy waits in a cove with a raft and paddle. When he sees Julia, he clasps his hands together and lifts them over his head in triumph.

Clancy takes Gabriel, then helps Julia and Cassie aboard. The planks of the raft creak. Cassie settles herself with Gabriel in her lap and one arm around Julia. Clancy pushes off. They float and spin away on a silver thread of water.

CHAPTER TWENTY-SEVEN

Cassie holds an egg in one hand. "Hit it on the bowl like this," she says to Missus, demonstrating. It's one of the precious four that Cassie has managed to procure, along with a quart of milk, by stopping a farmer with a cart on his way to First Market.

The egg splashes neatly into the bowl. Missus, wearing an apron, picks up the second egg and gingerly taps the shell. Cassie stifles a cluck of exasperation. The clumsiness that makes Missus sew crooked lines of stitches seems to afflict her in the kitchen, too.

"A little harder," says Cassie. "It ain't going to bite you."

Missus taps and the egg explodes, shell and all, into the bowl.

"Oh, dear!" Missus says.

Cassie uses part of a cracked shell to fish out the other pieces and hands Amanda a fork. "Whip it up good, now. Make little bubbles," she instructs.

Then Cassie shows her how to mix in a few spoonsful of cornmeal, a little sorghum, and enough milk to make a batter.

"Not too stiff, now. You got to be able to stir without the spoon standing up," says Cassie.

Missus pours the batter into a cast-iron skillet, then puts it on a shelf in the cookstove and closes the door. She looks up, face flushed, like a child who wants approval.

"Check and take it out when it be brown on top. The handle be hot, so wrap a towel around your hand," Cassie says.

Missus opens the door and squints at a pale circle of batter. "Is it brown enough now?"

"Naw. Should be more like the color of my hand."

"I hope I can do this without you."

"Miss Nell, she don't care what you fix, long as she have something to eat."

"When you come back, we'll have a feast."

Cassie goes into the dining room and returns with plates. Missus must not understand that she aims to keep going once she drops off the baby. For just a little while longer, she has to pretend that she's completely trustworthy. She tries to still her trembling hands by opening the oven door.

"Come see."

Amanda awkwardly wraps a towel around her hand, lifts the skillet, and grunts as she sets the pan on top of a folded towel on the kitchen table. She steps close as Cassie scoops out a portion of the cornbread for Nell. Cassie can hear her loud breathing. It's going to be a trial for Missus to learn an easy way with the stove, but it will take her mind off the baby she gave up.

The spoon clinks loudly against the plate.

"Careful, there! That's my mother's china," Amanda says.

Desperate for a quick distraction, Cassie says, "Miss Mildred, she never favored a simple supper like this. Always asking for something fancy."

Amanda flinches. "Well, what of it?"

"You ain't nothing like Miss Mildred. She a pinch-mouthed, mean thing. Master Carter better off with you."

Amanda thinks Cassie is just telling her what she wants to hear.

"And what if Master Carter doesn't come back?" Amanda snaps.

"Oh, I expect he will," says Cassie. "Just act like you be waiting for him all along."

Missus unties her apron and slumps in the kitchen chair. "Do you really mean that about Mildred?"

Cassie nods. "I know her since she a baby girl. You got your troubles, but you ain't mean like that."

Missus taps her fingers one at a time on the table, cycling through each one again and again. The apron bunches in her lap.

"Cassie?" she murmurs. "Hurry back. What will I do in this

big house, just me and Nell?"

Resisting the urge the shake Missus by her shoulders and tell her to stop stumbling around and to take charge of her own self, Cassie says, "You get used to it."

Missus scowls. The skin underneath her eyes looks all dark and smudged. Here she is, a white woman who can go anywhere and do anything, yet she's afraid to look after her own daughter and her own house. Cassie chooses her words carefully.

"The Lord bless you with a daughter. Do for her and the rest gonna come along with that."

CHAPTER TWENTY-EIGHT

At the back gate of the garden, Cassie cradles Jacob while Amanda goes back inside. Rays of sun are just beginning to pierce the morning fog. Nell waits, twisting her toe in the dirt, loudly exhaling so puffs of her breath cloud in front of her. The carriage has arrived to take all of them to the Richmond and Petersburg train depot. Amanda sent the driver to the end of the alley so they don't have to come out onto the street with the secret baby. Cassie and Jacob will catch the train and travel south from there. Yesterday, Amanda wrote to Mrs. Spencer to let her know of the departure date and that Cassie and Jacob would be traveling on their own.

> *February 25, 1865*
> *Dear Mrs. Spencer,*
> *I trust that this letter finds you well. I send news that my faithful servant, Cassie, will be personally delivering the package to you. It is safer for me to remain in Richmond at this time. Please let me know right away of the safe arrival of the package. These words cannot express my gratitude for your willingness to receive and keep this delivery. I hope it will bring you much joy.*
> *With every good wish,*
> *Mrs. Carter*

Amanda pushes open the back door, holding an extra hat for Jacob in one hand and a clean pillowcase in the other. Her hoop skirt teeters as she walks. It's the first time she has stepped out in public since she gave birth. Today of all days, she must look respectable. Cassie helped her into a corset. She could barely tighten the laces. Amanda has covered her tightly wound hair with a spoon bonnet that ties with navy blue ribbons and has wrapped her best wool shawl around herself.

"Take these," she tells Cassie, holding out the hat and pillowcase. "Pull the pillowcase over his feet if you need an extra blanket. He might get cold. He could get cold at any time."

Cassie patiently nods.

For the past day, Amanda has nervously packed a satchel for Jacob, putting in clean baby gowns, diapers, and every other piece of cloth that might possibly be useful to him. For food, Cassie put in apples, cooked potatoes, a jar of tomatoes, and even stale biscuits. At the market, she managed to procure a quart of milk and a bottle. A special pocket on the inside front of Cassie's dress contains her traveling pass.

To write the pass, Amanda went into the alcove off the parlor and opened Edwin's flip-top desk to look for a sheet of stationery from Carter Tobacco. She seldom goes in there, preferring to write letters at her lap desk. Edwin keeps his affairs tidily organized: a ledger in one cubbyhole, a pen in another, and stationery and envelopes in a third. As she sat in the stiff-backed wooden chair, she wondered how to word the pass to best protect Cassie and herself. The name and address from Carter Tobacco would show that Cassie had a legitimate owner with a business address in Richmond. The question was how long to make the pass valid. The post office clerk said the trip to the eastern coast of North Carolina would normally take four or five days, but with the wartime roads and torn-up railroad tracks, it might take more than a week. Amanda wanted to give Cassie enough time to get to North Carolina and back, but not extra. Underneath the date, she finally wrote,

My trusted family servant, Cassie, has my permission to travel with baby Jacob, who is white. The baby is an orphan who is going to be adopted by his aunt, Mrs. A.A. Spencer of Washington, North Carolina. Please allow them to travel unimpeded from the 26th of February, 1865 through the 26th of March, 1865.

Amanda opened the top drawer and looked for a paper with Edwin's full signature. She found a receipt for a shipment of tobacco, then pressed it against the window with the pass in front of it so she could trace the curly E in Edwin and the long tail on the end of the last r in Carter, forging his signature. Her own name on the pass would not carry the same weight.

From the bottom drawer of the desk, Amanda pulled two gold coins from Edwin's supply. Cassie would need money to pay for her ticket and possibly to bribe people along the way. Cassie had sewn a secret pocket into the hem of her dress, and would place the second coin in the toe of her boot, under the rag that kept it from sliding around.

Today, Cassie wears her Sunday dress and a threadbare wool cloak from Amanda that Cassie had to cut down so the bottom wouldn't drag along the ground. In the satchel, she brings an extra workday dress and a shawl. She also carries Mrs. Walker's Bible to leave with Jacob. Amanda wrote his first name and birth date—January 16, 1865—but did not sign her own name. The Spencers can fill in the rest however they want to.

The carriage wheels squeak as they roll down the south side of Church Hill to Main Street. The sun slants across brick building fronts, brightening them from maroon to crimson. Buds soften the stark outlines of the linden and maple tree branches. At Cary Street, they turn right, passing the city gas works. Next they pass the tobacco district in Shockoe Bottom, where Edwin has his warehouse. Most of the warehouses sit empty in late winter, puddles instead of wagons in front of their massive doors. As the carriage turns toward the railroad depot, they pass long, flat-bottomed riverboats jammed together in the Kanawha Canal, waiting to be loaded with munitions or barrels of flour from the Gallego mill.

Amanda holds Jacob against her, his head beneath her chin. Tears slide down her cheeks.

"Sad, sad Mama," says Nell, patting Amanda's arm. Amanda worries that she will sob aloud if she answers Nell, so she sniffs and nods. Cassie draws her shawl tightly around herself.

The carriage can't get close to the main entrance of the depot because so many military wagons have pulled up. The driver parks where he finds an open spot and helps them down. Gray-uniformed soldiers weave around Amanda and Cassie as their sergeant shouts at them to stay in formation.

Inside, more soldiers swirl around them as they look for a conductor. On the platform, ill men lie on blankets waiting for transport to the Receiving Hospital. Some moan. Nell clings to Cassie's dress. They see no other women anywhere.

When Amanda finally finds a railroad worker, he eyes her impatiently. The top of his cap and jacket are smeared with soot. "This is Cassie, my servant," says Amanda. "She is taking this white baby to North Carolina, where his aunt and uncle can look after him. His poor mother died bringing him into this world."

"Well, ma'am, this train is for soldiers. Soldiers only. Ain't no room for no nursemaid nigger and no baby."

"But they have to go. A family is waiting for them, and the baby needs their protection. He can't stay in Richmond. This is no place to keep a baby safe," says Amanda.

The conductor rubs together his hands and squints.

"We have the fare," says Amanda, holding out a fat stack of Confederate bills, more than the train should cost.

In one smooth motion, he takes the money and pockets it.

"They are going to Petersburg, then on to North Carolina."

"Them Yankees cut the Weldon line near Petersburg. No train until 30 miles south of there. Stagecoach is the only way out of Petersburg."

Amanda and Cassie exchange a glance.

"Mail car," he says, motioning to the rear of the train with his head, then walking away.

As they reach the steps, Cassie quickly hugs Nell and says, "Be good to your mama."

Cassie holds out her arms for the baby.

"Jacob," whispers Amanda, her eyes watering. "Jacob, Jacob, Jacob, my son. Goodbye, my beloved."

"You doing what you need to do. Master Edwin, he ain't gonna know nothing," says Cassie.

Amanda leans down and settles Jacob in Cassie's arms. She nuzzles his soft head, resting her hand against Cassie's back. The boniness of Cassie's frame surprises Amanda. Cassie smells like wood smoke from the cook stove. Then Amanda kisses Jacob on each cheek, on his forehead, and surrenders him.

CHAPTER TWENTY-NINE

Cassie and Jacob settle onto a torn bag in the mail car, displacing a dark-skinned man with a high forehead and a flat nose. He and about a dozen other Negroes sprawl on other bags or on the floor. Some of the windows are broken out. Cold, sooty air rushes in, but at least it airs out the stench of sweat and piss. Judging from the bloodstains on crumpled rags and on the floor, this car must have previously transported the wounded. Jacob stirs and Cassie rubs his back to quiet him. Soon, she'll have to try to pour milk into the bottle on this lurching train, and risk wasting some.

Ever since Cassie came to Richmond, she has dreamed about the day she would leave. Yet she never expected to be doing so with a white baby in her arms and a pass in her pocket. Instead of feeling joyful, she feels jittery. When she closes her eyes for a minute, her lids feel grainy. She jerks them back open.

The man with the flat nose introduces himself as a cook for a regiment of North Carolina Infantry that rides in the front of the train. His forearms look scarred from handling hot pots.

"Where you and that baby headed?"

"North Carolina. He going to live with his people. His mama died," says Cassie, delivering the speech she and Amanda rehearsed. "Where I got to go when I get off this train?"

The man adjusts his hat and lets out a low whistle.

"You in for a sight. Petersburg is tore up. Both sides dug in, shooting at each other. You best get out of there fast as you can."

Cassie tries not to let her nervousness show. The man puts the hat in front of his face and snoozes.

About an hour later, when they reach the Petersburg station, the railroad man swaggers through the car. The cook helps Cassie get off the train and steers her through hordes of soldiers to the station's front door. He points toward the steeple of a church.

"Stagecoach stop up there. You need help, look for colored womenfolk. Don't trust no soldiers. They like as not to try to sell you or put you to work cooking or washing. If you say that baby white, they just laugh."

Cassie thanks him and looks for a place where she can sit and feed Jacob. The ground in front of the station is occupied by men on stretchers, so she walks around the back of the building and sits on the bank of the Appomattox River. The wind cuts into her cheeks. She draws her cloak around herself and Jacob, leans him back in the crook of her arm, and slides the tip of the bottle into his mouth.

She hums a tune that she learned at the Scruggs plantation. *Hush little baby, don't say a word...* She remembers holding Miss Mildred as a baby in her freshly laundered gown. The edge of the bonnet made scallops across her tiny forehead. Cassie liked the hours in the rocking chair when Missus Scruggs left her alone with the baby's soft weight against her shoulder. Later, when Cassie had children of her own, she barely had ten minutes to rock them before one of the Scruggs women called for her.

After feeding Jacob, Cassie settles him in her lap. She pulls out a biscuit and opens the jar of tomatoes. The sooner she eats the tomatoes, the less chance she'll break the jar. She changes Jacob's diaper and sets him down, head propped up on the satchel, while she rinses the soiled diaper in the river. As soon as she can stop, she'll hang it out to dry.

Before she continues, she prays that Jesus will give her a sign that the journey will be safe. The water slides by with nothing to tell her. She sighs and stands up, holding Jacob.

As she begins to walk toward the church, caissons and military wagons rumble through the main street. Spindly trees, their limbs beginning to bud, line the route. At the back door of a three-story stone courthouse building, a clerk with an unkempt brown beard and eyes like rain clouds squints at her when she asks where the stagecoaches stop and where they go.

"I ain't got no business with no runaways."

Cassie pulls out her pass and says, "This here baby, he white."

The man unfolds the pass, frowns, and runs his finger across the Carter Tobacco name, leaving a faint smudge of dirt. Then he hands it back to Cassie.

"All right, then. Where you headed? Petersburg to Tarboro, North Carolina, leaves four o'clock a.m. on Tuesdays and Fridays. Boydton stage leaves here in about an hour," he says. "Stops in Dinwiddie, McKenna, Alberta, Lombardy Grove. Part of the road may be washed out, and there's no telling what them armies are up to, but you may get through."

Cassie recognizes the name Dinwiddie. She accompanied Missus Scruggs and the other women to the courthouse square many times as they shopped at the stores there. Clancy sometimes drove them in the wagon. If she found her way to Baker's store, she might be able to get to the Scruggs place—and to her children. She had planned to drop off Jacob first and look for them afterwards, but Jacob could wait to go to North Carolina. He wouldn't know the difference.

"Dinwiddie, sir," she says, handing over a stack of Confederate bills that Missus said would be about the right fare.

"You're short five dollars," says the man.

Cassie holds out another bill and hopes it's enough. He may be overcharging her, but she can't read the bills or count so she has no way of knowing.

"Go out to the stable and set there 'til the stage comes," says the man, carefully grasping the bill by its edge so his fingers won't touch a colored woman's hand.

After mumbling an obligatory, "Thank you, sir," Cassie turns her back to him as quickly as possible and hurries away.

CHAPTER THIRTY

"Mama?" Nell says, pushing Amanda's shoulder. "Mama, wake up!"

Amanda rolls over and opens her eyes. Nell's cheek is textured from the pillow and her hair sprawls in wild corkscrews above the neck of her sleeping gown. She carries her doll, Rose, in the crook of her arm.

"Good morning," says Amanda, trying to sound cheerful when all she wants to do is stay in bed, arms empty since Jacob left more than a week before. Her breasts still ache and leak milk. She keeps waking in the night, listening for Jacob's soft breath, though she moved the cradle back into Nell's room the morning he left. Nell puts Rose to sleep in the cradle now. Amanda knows she should take out the baby linens and wash them, but once she does, she will lose the last trace of Jacob's sweet, milky scent.

Amanda gets up, goes to her washbasin, and wets a cloth. She needs to remember to refill the pitcher later this morning. She closes her eyes and wipes her face.

Then she tells Nell, "Your turn to wash up."

Nell sticks out her tongue. "Cassie always combs my hair first."

"Well, I do things this way. Wash up first. Then we'll do your hair."

Nell takes the washcloth and balls it up. "It's cold. Cassie doesn't bring cold water."

"I haven't had time to heat the water this morning."

"When is she coming back?"

"Not until spring, maybe when we see the daffodils."

"I want it to be spring now."

"Well, it will come faster if you hold still while I wash your face. Now, go get your comb."

Nell squirms while Amanda wets the comb and goes to work. After Nell's hair is untangled and Amanda has helped her into a dress and stockings, Amanda returns to her room. She slips out of her nightdress and puts on her corset, straining to tighten the lace in back. That was always Cassie's job. Then Amanda struggles into her stockings, petticoats, and calico work dress. As she turns to go downstairs, she looks down and realizes she needs to pick up her chamber pot to dump in the privy.

By the time Amanda goes out to pull up a bucket from the well, a light drizzle is spattering her shoulders. Crocuses the size of Nell's pinky finger are still closed in the early morning but will open if it clears up later. The camellias will soon bloom, bringing their welcome pink. In later March, Amanda can expect bright clusters of the daffodils that she planted when she first moved in, before vegetables took precedence over flowers.

With Cassie gone, there's barely time for Amanda to pause to admire the garden. She needs to carry in wood and start the fire in the stove. Then she must turn her attention to cooking.

As Amanda builds up the fire, Nell comes into the kitchen, her stockings sliding on the bare floor.

"I'm hungry."

"I'm making breakfast."

"You're taking too long."

"Shh!" Amanda hisses into the stove.

"I'm hungry," Nell repeats.

Amanda stands up, slams the oven door shut, and wheels around to face her daughter. "Why can't you just wait a few minutes?"

"Cassie never made me wait."

"Cassie this, Cassie that! I'm tired of hearing about Cassie! I'm the one who is your mother."

"I like Cassie better! She isn't always slow and cross with me."

Amanda feels the heat rising in her face and her throat

tightening. "Go back up to your room! I won't have you speaking to me like this."

Nell stares at Amanda, not moving. Then she pats her doll's head and says to the doll, "Don't worry. I won't let Mama be mean to you."

"Go to your room right now!" Amanda shouts, advancing so she can strong-arm the girl up the stairs if need be.

"She's the meanest mama ever," says Nell to the doll.

"GO!" Amanda shouts.

Nell turns, tucks Rose against her chest, and races up the stairs.

Alone with breakfast still to make, Amanda slumps in the kitchen chair. Yelling and banishing Nell reminds her of how Aunt Margaret used to treat her. But why is Nell so impudent? Amanda is doing her best to fight off her sadness about giving up Jacob and also remember all the chores she has to do. Maybe it was a mistake letting Cassie go away with Jacob. Everything ran so smoothly when she was here.

Amanda needs time to calm down and think of how to be more patient with Nell. She wishes she could go out for a walk but she can't leave such a young girl alone in the house. It's too chilly to sit in the garden. Pacing around the kitchen, she sees the narrow opening to Cassie's room behind the pantry, walks in, and blinks at the dimness. A small window at the top of the back wall lets in a bit of light, but otherwise there is nothing to soften the bare walls. Cassie's worn dress hangs on a nail behind the door. Amanda presses the fabric to her nose. There's still a faint trace of Cassie's smoky odor.

"What am I going to do?" she whispers, as if Cassie can hear her.

What a small room Cassie occupied all alone. Amanda sits on the pallet, heedless of a lifetime of being told to stay away from dank, filthy slave rooms. This room is swept clean except for a strange pile of chestnuts, a shred of green cloth, and a leather strap in one corner.

Amanda lies down on the pallet. Her feet hang off the end so she curls on her side. She pulls the blanket over herself. It's scratchy. Careful stitches close up several moth holes. Cassie found a way to make the best of what she was provided. Amanda will have to learn how to do that. She closes her eyes and tries to still her cartwheeling thoughts.

She remembers Cassie tending the vegetables, giving Nell little jobs to do—weeding under the tomatoes or carrying a small watering can. If Nell pulled up a vegetable stem instead of a weed or watered her feet instead of the plants, Cassie never spoke sharply. She either laughed or gently corrected the girl. No wonder Nell wants Cassie to come back. From now on, Amanda vows to make herself stop acting like "the meanest mama ever."

Standing up and smoothing her dress, she goes back into the kitchen, measures out a cup of rice, puts it in a pot, adds two cups of water, and begins to heat it on the stove. She remembers Cassie's instructions: cover the pot when the water starts to boil, then move it to a cooler part of the cooktop so it doesn't keep boiling furiously. Into another pot she places some dried apples and water so they will simmer into applesauce.

When everything is ready, Amanda prepares a breakfast tray for Nell. She scoops the steaming food into two painted china bowls from her mother's set instead of the everyday earthenware. Then she drapes her cloak over her shoulders and goes out back to find a flower or a bit of greenery to put in a vase the way Cassie would. Underneath the magnolia, it smells of damp earth. The seed pods that once held red berries now look like dry, brown husks. She kicks one with the toe of her boot, then walks back towards the rear wall. It's not quite time for the leaves to brighten and sprout, so she breaks off a sprig of rain-spattered holly. Its pointed leaves look like little crowns. Maybe she can tell Nell one of the fairy tales about kings and queens that she remembers her own mother reciting to her.

Amanda closes her eyes and wanders through flickering memories from when her mother was still alive, speaking in her musical, English accent. "Mandy," she called Amanda. No one had ever used that nickname since. Mandy was another girl in another life, disconnected from the grown and overwhelmed Amanda.

Amanda arranges the food and the holly, then carries it up to Nell's room. She walks in without knocking. Nell is sprawled facedown on the bed, her doll next to her.

"Go away," she tells her mother, not turning over.

"I brought you breakfast," Amanda says, setting the tray on top of Nell's bureau.

"I'm not hungry anymore."

"Nell, I spoke too harshly to you. I'm sorry."

Nell grunts.

"Your rice and applesauce are still warm. I put a surprise on the tray, too."

Nell rolls over, her eyes red and nose running. It's all Amanda's fault that she looks so disheveled and miserable. In Amanda's preoccupation with what to do about Jacob, the girl in front of her—thin arms, blotchy cheeks, wrinkled dress—became an afterthought. Amanda wants to pull her close and tell her how much she loves her, but it would be too much all at once, like giving her real tea with rich cream and sugar after months of in-adequate substitutes. Nell would just push her away.

"I brought my mother's china upstairs, even though we have to be extra careful with it. I know you like the pretty roses on the bowls," Amanda says, standing next to the bed. "It's not the season for flowers yet but I found something green for you."

Nell blinks. Amanda opens the bureau drawer, pulls out one of the handkerchiefs that Cassie laundered and pressed, and hands it to Nell.

"Ready?" Amanda asks, picking up the tray. "You can share your food with Rose."

Nell wipes her eyes, sits up, and takes the bowl of rice. As she begins alternately eating and holding the spoon in front of Rose's mouth, Amanda sits beside her on the bed and says, "My Mummy once told me a story about a king and queen who were sad because they went for a long time without having children. Then their wish came true with a girl named Briar Rose. Would you like to hear?"

Nell sniffles, then nods.

CHAPTER THIRTY-ONE

Cassie climbs down from the stagecoach in Dinwiddie. She feels slightly sick from the swaying, lurching ride, but at least Jacob slept most of the way. He's calm now but soon he will be hungry. In the long afternoon shadows, Cassie recognizes the boxy courthouse building painted white, plus the tall poplars and grassy lawn of the village square. She walks briskly towards Baker's store so she can keep warm and buy more milk for Jacob. If she can't find a ride to the Scruggs place, she can at least try to find a kind family to take pity on a white baby and let them stay in their barn or another outbuilding. Fatigue and excitement about being so near her children make her light-headed.

Cassie circles to the back of the store, where three tied-up horses nicker. Dusk makes the air grainy, but she welcomes the darkness. Even though she has a pass, she wants to arrive at the Scruggs place at a time she can go straight to the stable and look for Clancy. There's no telling what Master and Missus Scruggs will do if they see her again. They might even blame her for Miss Mildred's death, even though Cassie can tell them how Miss Mildred writhed and moaned while the midwife helplessly rubbed her lower back and urged her to push out the baby.

Inside the store, Cassie holds Jacob close. He has fallen asleep, his head resting against her shoulder. Cassie nods to the clerk, a young man she does not recognize. It may be one of Mr. Baker's sons. She waits until all the white customers have been served and then asks for a package of crackers and a quart of milk, paying with money that Amanda gave her.

She follows a stout Negro man with two burlap bags heading out to a horse and cart.

"Evening," she greets him softly.

He tips his battered felt hat to her.

"You have a notion to help me and this baby?"

He eyes her carefully, then sets the bags in the back of the cart.

"Ain't seen you before," says the man.

"Passing through," says Cassie.

"That's a young 'un you got there, all right."

"I got a pass," she says, and tells him about the orphaned baby.

"I want no trouble," he says. "You ain't lying to me?"

"I got a pass," she repeats and pulls it out to show him, though it's unlikely he would know how to read.

"Where you headed?"

"Scruggs place. You know where it at?"

He nods. "Going to the Doyle place. Scruggs on the way."

After he helps her and Jacob into the cart, he climbs into the driver's seat and clucks to the horse. They roll down the road as the setting sun bulges behind the tree limbs. Cassie wonders if she should be taking such a risk. Missus expects her to go straight to North Carolina. If she gets in trouble here, no telling what Missus will do, especially if harm comes to Jacob. What will she find at the Scruggs place, anyway? Maybe Clancy and her children are no longer there. Instead of finding friendly folks in the quarters, she may find a busybody who rushes to tell Master Scruggs that she has returned. He could send her back to Richmond, beat her, or rip up her pass and force her to work there again. Still, she has a chance to go there now and she doesn't want to waste it.

The cart hits a bump and the man looks over his shoulder to check on her. Cassie waves her hand to reassure him and is grateful he doesn't ask questions. Jacob stirs but she pats him to put him back to sleep. They ride in silence.

By the time they reach the entrance road to the farm, stars scatter the sky like a handful of corn tossed to chickens. The moon will light her way down the road to the stable. She thanks the man and sets off, staying to the edge of the road. Even if

Clancy is not there, she and Jacob should be able to shelter in the stable overnight. Her feet remember the terrain, even with a satchel and a child weighing her down. This is where she walked with her own mother, whose dress flapped beside Cassie's outstretched hand. Cassie's footsteps crunch as they churn the cold dirt. Jacob rocks in her arms. A single lantern hangs by the stable door, and she walks to it.

CHAPTER THIRTY-TWO

Amanda goes out to the back porch and scrapes scorched bits of cornbread onto the ground. Just once, she'd like to make a pan of tender, light bread the way Cassie showed her, but something always goes wrong. It's raw on one side and burned on the other, or lumpy all over. She puts the pan on the top step and pours in a cup of water. It can soak while she and Nell plant their first seedlings.

She leans against the handrail and inhales the scent of cold earth. Clouds blotch the horizon, and they need to do their work before it rains. Maybe the spring will bring better news about the war. General Sherman is still in the midst of his cruel Carolinas Campaign, which captured Columbia, South Carolina, and left it in flames. His troops have swept into North Carolina, looting anything they take a fancy to along the way. She wonders if Little Washington will be safe. According to the *Daily Dispatch*, Confederate General Joseph Johnston is doing all he can to stop Sherman, but Sherman's army is a juggernaut. At least Edwin hasn't yet started a spring campaign in the Shenandoah Valley.

Her latest letter is ready to mail. With Jacob gone, she no longer has to agonize about what to say. She longs for the sweet scent of Edwin's pipe tobacco in the parlor, for the starched plane of his freshly ironed shirt against the side of her cheek. From now on, he deserves her sweetest attention.

> *March 1, 1865*
> *Dear Edwin,*
> *I set myself to write you a few lines to let you know Nell and I are well. I hope these remarks find you in the same blessings of good health. What a long winter it has been in Richmond! How glad we are to see the first small signs of spring in the trees and in our own garden. We have crocuses*

and little green shoots of peppermint coming up. I know that the season has been ever longer for you, suffering as you have through one of the coldest winters that anyone can remember. I hope you feel the ever-brightening sun strengthening you as you prepare for the spring campaigns that must inevitably come.

Nell is getting mighty tall. We will be ready to plant a few vegetable seedlings soon. The city suffers on, but we had the good fortune of coming across a brass band at Capitol Square last week. The bright music gave us all encouragement.

We will rejoice in the time that you may return to the care of your family. May that time come soon.

Devotedly,

Amanda

Nell comes downstairs in her sleeping gown just as Amanda is climbing out of the root cellar with a sack of the dry peas that she saved from last year.

"You need to eat breakfast and get dressed lickety-split today," Amanda says. "We're going to start planting."

The part of the cornbread that didn't burn fell apart, so she hands Nell a plate of crumbs and a fork.

Nell wrinkles her nose. "When is Cassie coming back?"

"Daffodil time, remember?" says Amanda quickly.

Nell pokes at the cornbread.

"Pour some of this on it," she says, handing Nell a spoonful of sorghum molasses. The crumbs stick all over the spoon, but at least Nell takes a bite.

After Amanda helps Nell get dressed, they go to the compost pile near the back wall. Using a spade, Amanda digs up dirt from the vegetable patch and asks Nell to sprinkle in a bucketful of compost. The familiar work of turning soil relaxes her.

Amanda remembers something sing-songy that her mother

used to recite. Maybe Nell will be more likely to stay by her side if she has something interesting to do.

"I know a rhyme about a bush."

"Is it your Mummy's rhyme?"

"Yes, it is."

"How come I never see her? Is she with my Daddy?"

"No. She passed away when I was girl not much older than you are," Amanda says, fighting back the stab of sudden tears.

"What's passing away?"

"When someone dies. Their body stops working and they go up to heaven, where we can't see them anymore."

"Did my Daddy pass away?" Nell barely remembers Edwin from his furlough more than a year before.

"No, he's just far away for a long time," Amanda says and then begins the rhyme to end Nell's questions. "Here we go round the mulberry bush," she sings, trying to imitate her mother's accent by pronouncing mulberry like "mul-bree."

"That sounds funny," says Nell.

"That's what she sounded like. She came from a place called England, far across the water. I never saw the big water she talked about. I've heard it can hold boats much bigger than the ones on the James River."

"What does my Daddy sound like?"

Amanda tries to remember Edwin's voice. He always enunciated thoroughly, his baritone rich and resonant in his chest. "Pretty much like any gentleman around Richmond. Not funny like my mother."

"Will I hear him again?"

"I hope so."

Amanda makes up a new verse to the song. "This is the way we plant our peas, plant our peas…"

She hands Nell a trowel so they can transfer their soil-compost mix to two long flower boxes. Amanda carries the flower boxes to the back porch and brings out the sack of seeds. Pulling the handle of a wooden spoon through the dirt in the flower box, she makes a shallow ditch. Nell carefully sprinkles in the dry peas and they both crumble handfuls of dirt lightly over the top. Then Amanda pours water through Nell's fingers to gently water the seeds, just as Nate taught her.

Amanda places the flower boxes in the sunny back window in the kitchen, where they can watch the tiny plants start to grow.

"Why do we put the garden inside?" says Nell.

"We have to protect the plants. It still might get too cold, especially at night."

Nell peers into the flower boxes. "Where are the plants?"

"The plants are inside the seeds. They'll come up. When they are strong enough, we'll move them outside."

Nell looks out the window. "I want it to be daffodil time now."

"Soon," Amanda says as she reheats yesterday's Indian pea soup for lunch. They eat in the kitchen now because the stove warms the room, and it saves Amanda the trouble of carrying everything into the dining room.

Nell brings the first spoonful of soup to her mouth and then abruptly lets the spoon clatter down on the table.

"What's that?" she asks pointing.

Something gray streaks across the floor and then along the wall behind the table.

"Oh, no. A mouse!" says Amanda.

Nell starts eating again.

"We have to get it out!" Amanda stands and lifts her skirt to keep the mouse from running under it.

"Hickory dickory dock." Nell chants another nursery rhyme that Amanda taught her, unfazed. "The mouse ran up the clock."

"Help me!" says Amanda, brandishing a broom. She opens the back door, letting in a gust of damp air. Shrieking, she and Nell chase the mouse outside.

"Goodbye, Mister Mouse!" says Nell, as if he's an honored guest.

Amanda laughs so hard she has to wipe her eyes.

CHAPTER THIRTY-THREE

Cassie lightly taps on the door to the stable. When there is no answer, she taps again, a little louder this time. She hears footsteps, then a click as the door unlatches.

Clancy picks up the lantern and stares at her, his greenish eyes wide. His pale brown cheeks droop more than she remembers. Lines cross his forehead. Yet his compact body looks as lean and muscular as it ever did.

"Glory be!" he says softly. "What you doing out there, woman? And with a baby?"

"Shh," says Cassie. "Let me in."

He opens his arms and she steps towards him, holding Jacob against her hip. She uses her free arm to circle his waist and leans her chin on his shoulder. Clancy smells of leather, horse sweat, and a grassy aroma she had all but forgotten.

"Sit yourself down," he says, pointing to a broken chair in the tack room. He slides the satchel off her shoulder. She pulls a blanket from it so she can reposition Jacob on the floor.

"Got some water? And what you got to eat?" she says.

He goes outside and returns with a tin cup of water, a wet cloth, and a biscuit.

She thanks him and sits back, easing her feet out of Missus's old boots. He seems to be waiting for her to speak, turning his hat around and around in his hands. Gray now threads his closely cropped hair. Cassie remembers the shape of the cheeks she once held between her hands. She looks down, marveling at how her fingers know exactly how sharp his bones felt. Such a long time ago.

"Tell me true. Have you run away?" he finally asks.

"No."

"That baby yours?"

"No."

He waits while she rubs her feet and explains.

Then she asks, "How can I see our young'uns?"

He sucks his teeth. The lantern throws up strange shadows on the rough boards of the tack room walls. A horse stamps in one of the stalls.

"Not so safe for you here," he says.

"Mm-hm."

"I could hide you for a couple of days, but then you got to move on. Master Scruggs find you, no telling what he do, even with your pass."

Jacob begins stirring and Cassie jumps up to tend to him. After he drinks his bottle and she changes his diaper, she holds him in her lap. Jacob seems mesmerized by the lantern.

"Julia, she all grown up, got a baby of her own now," says Clancy.

Cassie gasps. "She got herself a man, too?"

"She won't talk about how she got the baby girl. Katie, she called. She a right plump little thing. Must be 'cause Julia's doing most of the cooking up at the house. Kind of taken over from Old Jenny. She stay up there at the house."

"What about our boy?"

"Gabriel, he real tall. Over my head now, with big hands and feet, like a puppy dog. Ain't got much to say to me or nobody else, but has a way with horses. My right hand, you could say."

"Where he at?"

Clancy looks down at his hands. "With Molly. He stay with us and our own three children. Uh, well, I..."

"What you supposed to do? Me sold off like that."

Clancy goes back to turning his hat, then says, "Got to tell you something else."

"What?" says Cassie, leaning back, already exhausted.

"He call her Mama. He don't remember you. Oh, he do at first, walking all around the place with a blanket calling, 'Mama,

Mama,' and so sad. I tell him to stop calling 'cause you can't hear him no more. Say you still love him but you just can't hear. When I move into Molly's cabin, well…"

Cassie absently rubs Jacob's back, her palm going around and around. All that time she spent picturing Gabriel's plump, coffee-colored face each night and praying next to the shrine she made for him—and he thinks someone else is his mother.

"You left. Not your fault, but you left. He better off this way," says Clancy.

"Not to me."

"That's the way of it."

Cassie silently prays for forbearance, her visions of sweeping up each child in her arms wavering like the lantern's light.

After a few minutes, she asks, "Where can a body get some rest?"

Clancy helps her up the ladder to a little nook above the tack room, then hands Jacob to her. He climbs up the ladder with two blankets and spreads them. Cassie lies down, putting Jacob between her and the wall. When Clancy reaches for her, she nestles against him. Such a long time ago.

"Never stopped loving you," he whispers. "Never thought this old body would see you again."

"Got to rest now," she says before falling asleep in his arms. While it's still dark out, Jacob cries out. After Cassie feeds him and lies back down, she is finally ready to turn towards Clancy. All the remembered gestures and passions return as if they are once again stealing away into the fields after dark, her body spread out like a blanket, soft in the dark beneath his hands.

Chapter Thirty-four

Amanda pushes aside the wooden plank on top of the root cellar and lights a candle. Carefully, holding up her dress so she won't trip, she descends the ladder. When she reaches the dirt floor at the bottom, she waves away cobwebs and does a quick inventory. Only a half-barrel each of apples and potatoes remain. Spring greens from the garden won't be ready for another month or so.

With a pencil, she writes down cornmeal, flour, and eggs (if available) on the edge of the *Daily Dispatch* and tears off the piece of paper. Then she composes a shopping list in her head, throwing in items she is sure never to find: ham, butter, sugar, and freshly baked rolls. She remembers leisurely breakfasts at Uncle Chester and Aunt Margaret's, where the slaves brought her coffee, hot biscuits, butter, and ham. They silently walked over to refill her mug, and to clear the plates away. She never thought about how they carried in water and firewood, rinsed dishes in a pan and poured the water out into the yard, as she does now in Cassie's absence. All those tasks took place away from the table where she sat in front of the silver place settings and fine linen cloth from England that the "servants" washed and ironed.

Nell sits on the steps in the entry hall, waiting for Amanda. She leans over her doll and tells her, "Walk down the stairs like a big girl. No asking about the baby or Cassie. Mama won't say where they are."

Amanda hasn't said anything about Cassie to Nell because she has heard no news. Mrs. Spencer is supposed to send a letter as soon as Jacob arrives, but frequent trips to the post office turn up nothing. When Amanda gave Cassie permission to go to North Carolina, she didn't count on her own endless loops of worry about the dangers of having Cassie and Jacob move among two warring armies. If Cassie makes it back safely, she deserves the chance to find her own children.

Amanda hands Nell a shawl, then wraps one around her own shoulders. They walk down 26th Street, looking for signs of spring. Sharp-eyed Nell finds pigweed sprouting up between the cobblestones, untrammeled by hooves and wheels. After such long confinement, Amanda appreciates the scent of wood smoke rising from chimneys around Church Hill, the glint of puddles in the street, even the military supply wagons on their way to and from the front in Petersburg. It makes her feel a part of the world again instead of a container for an ever larger and more cumbersome secret.

Bright sun warms the stone stairs as Amanda and Nell climb down to Main Street. By noon, it may be warm enough for both of them to be able to drape their shawls across their arms. Not a single cloud mottles the deep, cerulean blue of the sky.

Three blocks from the market stalls on 17th Street, Nell begins to sulk and drag her feet. Amanda looks back over her shoulder and tells her to come along. How was Cassie so patient with the dawdling, distractible girl? Amanda folds her arms across her waist and waits. Her dress is still a bit tight, but it should soon fit properly again. A cabriolet and two horses and carts go by before Nell finally catches up. Amanda reaches out her hand, trying to clasp the girl's thin, skittery fingers. They walk together for a few minutes, but in the middle of a block on Main Street, Nell begins to lag behind once more. Amanda sighs and walks slowly ahead, waiting for Nell to catch up.

On the opposite side of the street, walking with her head down, a woman like Cassie heads towards them. Amanda looks up and studies the woman. She wears a dark brown dress with an apron tied around the waist and a headscarf dyed indigo blue. The woman is the same size as Cassie, but she walks with a slight limp.

Could Cassie be back in Richmond so soon, with no word from Mrs. Spencer? Is she injured? Maybe Mrs. Spencer's letter was lost. Just then, the woman lifts her head for a moment, and Amanda sees a different face, with a pointy nose and a large scar above her right eye.

When Amanda turns back again to look for Nell, she can't find her. Perhaps she slipped through the iron gate of the house next to them. Trembling, she flings it open.

"Nell? Nell? Where have you gotten to?"

Boxwood hedges line a path around the house.

Amanda runs back out to the spot where she last saw Nell, looking up and down the street, still calling for her.

To her left, a small figure moving so fast that she looks like a blur dashes into the street. "Cassie!" Nell shouts.

Then Nell screams in a shrill, unnatural pitch that Amanda has never heard before. Amanda leans forward and begins to run, her long legs too slow for her frantic body.

"Whoa, there!" someone yells.

A red-faced soldier totters beside a wagon filled with ammunition, both hands on the reins of a bucking horse.

Amanda runs to the other side of the wagon and stops with a great heave of her chest. Nell's broken body lies facedown on the cobblestones, her neck crushed by the wheel that rolled over it.

A pool of blood gathers under Nell's mouth. Amanda tries to lift her daughter, but there's too much blood, too much damage to the small body. It's too late to call for a doctor, too late even to comfort Nell here on the cobblestones.

Amanda screams without words.

A crowd gathers around Amanda, blocking the air, blocking the sky. Everything whirls. Nell was right beside her not more than five minutes ago. If Amanda turns her head and looks over her shoulder, maybe it will all be a mistake, a bad dream, like the one about Edwin's face as shriveled as an overripe pumpkin.

It's all her fault. Why did she grow impatient and walk ahead? Of course Nell wanted to run off when she thought she saw Cassie. It was Cassie who took care of her every day, and Cassie whom she missed.

Amanda lies flat in the street, one hand on Nell's back, the other still clutching her empty market basket. Grit and pebbles press into her cheek. She has no breath to talk.

A strange man with a cloud of whiskers looms over her and asks where her family lives. Voices murmur behind him.

"Please, no," Amanda says, unsure she is making sense. "Let me stay with her." If only Nell would come up behind her calling, "Mama! Mama!"

The man says, "Ma'am, you can't stay here in the street. You need the aid of your family. Where may I take you?"

"Reverend Walker, Franklin and 26th," she manages to croak, then closes her eyes. Something metallic clanks above her head, and someone lifts her into a wagon. She feels the floorboards sag under her as someone else climbs up and places a small bundle next to her. It must be Nell, wrapped in a kind stranger's shawl. She rolls over and puts her arm around the bundle. The wagon jolts forward, making Amanda's head bounce against the floor as it rumbles along. Lying on her back, all Amanda sees is a sheet of the unnaturally blue sky with no edges and no bottom. The lurching ride makes her dizzy.

The wagon stops. The man with the whiskers steps down and knocks loudly on Mrs. Walker's door. Hinges creak.

"Good morning, sir," says Lucy.

"We need help," he says. "There's been a terrible accident!"

Amanda lies still as Lucy comes out and cries, "Lord have mercy!"

Amanda feels the man and Lucy lifting her up. A sob threatens to erupt from Amanda, powerful as whitewater in the river, but she keeps her eyes closed. Once she opens them, she will have to surrender Nell's broken, lifeless body and say goodbye to her forever.

Chapter Thirty-Five

When Cassie wakes, Clancy has left the loft. Morning light leaks through the spaces between the boards. Jacob sleeps peacefully on the blanket next to her. Though her back aches from yesterday's journey, she hurries down the ladder. She has to force herself not to fling open the stable door and run through the slave quarters shouting for her children. All she can do is whisper their once-familiar names to the horses, each one a scratch in her throat.

After retying her headscarf, she digs in the satchel for Julia's hair ribbon and wraps it around her wrist. She cracks open the door. Flies buzz in, but she shoos them. She pushes the chair into the back of the tack room and waits. It's strange to have this idle time. If only she had brought something to sew. Instead, she pulls out the Bible and opens to the Gospel of John. There is barely enough light to see the page.

She points her forefinger at the page and slowly sounds out, "*In the b-b-b-eeee-gin-ning...*" Every word that she can now read feels like a divine gift. She concentrates so hard that she startles when someone pushes open the door, bathing the room in bright light. Quickly closing the book, she places her flat hand above her forehead like a visor.

A coltish young woman in a brown dress the color of wren feathers stands in front of her, a baby in her arms. The skin on her face is like tea lightened with lots of milk. The woman bites her lower lip and squints into the room. Her face has lost its roundness, but Cassie remembers rubbing and kissing that forehead, wiping down that neck, braiding the hair now hidden beneath a pale yellow kerchief.

"Mama? Mama! It's really you?" says Julia.

Cassie stands and holds out the old hair ribbon, then folds Julia and the baby in her arms. Julia's chin grazes the top of Cassie's head. Cassie sobs while Clancy comes in and quietly shuts the door behind him.

Julia steps away and holds up the baby. "Meet your grandbaby, Katie. I call her that 'cause it sounds like Cassie. Born last spring right after planting time."

She hands Cassie the baby and smiles while Cassie holds her close and coos at her. The little girl's broad cheeks look pale as turnips, and her dark hair curls into ringlets but doesn't kink. Her gums show two bottom teeth.

Up in the loft, Jacob cries.

"Your papa tell you about the baby I got with me?" Cassie asks, handing Katie back and getting to her feet.

Julia nods.

Cassie climbs up and brings Jacob down.

"He a young thing! Healthy, too, it seem," says Julia.

"Yes, indeed, and hungry," says Cassie, reaching for a bottle.

Julia circles the room with her baby, shaking her head. "You here again. Here."

"I think about seeing you and Gabriel again since the day Miss Mildred call me away," says Cassie.

Julia walks over to Cassie and rubs Cassie's neck. Cassie leans back and feels her knotted muscles begin to ease.

When Jacob finishes his bottle, Cassie sets him down on a blanket and says, "Let me hold my grandbaby some more."

Julia stands. "No time. Missus Scruggs probably looking for me right now. 'Julia! I need tea! I need breakfast!' That woman can't do a thing for herself. Helpless as one of these babies."

"I remember," says Cassie, then laughs softly.

Julia holds Katie in one arm and picks up the pile of Jacob's diapers from the corner. "Doing a wash today. You not leaving yet, is you?"

Cassie smiles so wide she thinks her cheeks will crack. "This time, Lord willing, I ain't."

After Julia leaves, Cassie turns to Clancy and asks, "Where

Gabriel at?"

"With Master Pete, but he be back this afternoon."

"Master Pete? He all grown now?"

"A grown man."

"Not fighting?"

"No, he pay someone to go in his place."

"Of course he do."

"Well, Master Bobby, he go. Killed at Gettysburg. A shame, really. He the nicest one."

Cassie rubs her hands on her dress. "Your woman know I'm here?"

"No. The less folks know, the better."

"She don't ask where you stay last night?" she asks, elbowing him playfully.

"Sometimes I stay up here when the horses need something," Clancy says and picks up his hat. "I need to see to a carriage wheel. Try to keep that baby from crying too loud. Someone walk by and hear him, we done for. I send Gabriel soon as I can."

"What you gonna tell him?"

"A woman want to see him."

"A woman. Just a woman."

Clancy's face tightens. "He can't know all that."

"Well, I gonna tell him what I want to tell him."

"Think about it first," he says, and walks out.

CHAPTER THIRTY-SIX

Wrapping a black veil around her face, Amanda sets out to visit Nell's grave, as she has every day since the burial the week before. Reverend Walker performed the graveside service in Hollywood Cemetery. Mrs. Walker, Lucy, and two soldiers who were almost finished with their convalescence accompanied them.

Standing on a bluff overlooking the James, Reverend Walker was like a scarecrow with a black robe flapping on his reedy body. Wisps of gray hair wobbled across his forehead, and his eyes sank into his sallow cheeks. Yet his voice came forth melodiously. *"Jesus said, 'I am the resurrection and the life. He who believes in Me will live, even though he dies; and whoever lives and believes in Me will never die."*

Amanda bent her head so far down that all she could see was the hem of the black dress Mrs. Walker had given her. The ground opened like a scar to receive the tiny coffin while the words of the closing hymn blew up into the clouds.

Today, yellow forsythia buds brighten Church Hill like sparks, but it's still cool enough for a shawl. Amanda keeps her head down as she climbs down the stairs to Main Street and crosses Shockoe Creek on a rickety wooden bridge. She walks into the Post Office on 11th Street and waits in line for a chance to hear the clerk tell her yet again that he is sorry, Mrs. Carter, nothing today. Nothing from Mrs. Spencer telling her that Jacob has safely arrived. Nothing from Edwin. She sent Edwin a telegram the day after Nell died, but he has not answered.

Shoulders hunched, Amanda walks back out to the street. To her right, up a steep, grassy hill, a Confederate flag waves on one side of the capitol building, a Virginia flag on the other. She continues past a bank and a hotel where carriages wait, waving away a driver who is looking for a fare. At the city outskirts, peaked silhouettes of white military tents zigzag across the horizon. Smoke from the soldiers' cooking fires spirals up.

She wills herself to keep moving. If she stops, she is sure to relive Nell running, the flash of white, the scream, and then the awful silence that followed. Shame wells up along with her tears. How often had she let the new baby growing inside her push Nell out of her lap? Too frequently, she told Nell to look for Cassie, or go get her doll, or leave her alone.

Nell's life started out with such joy. Amanda remembers the first time she felt Nell on her chest right after she was born. Though Nell's face was still mottled with blood, Amanda instantly wrapped her arms around the little creature and felt flooded with love. Then Edwin tiptoed in, hat off, hair mussed, eyes wide. The awe of greeting his new baby rendered him speechless. He bent over the baby and stroked her still-damp scalp with one hand. When he looked up again, his cheeks shone with tears.

Yet in the weeks that followed, Amanda found it easier to hand Nell over to Cassie's practiced arms than to fumble through a diaper change or her futile attempts to stop Nell from crying. Cassie comforted the baby effortlessly.

Turning south and trudging towards the river, Amanda berates herself for letting everything go so terribly wrong. Through her heedlessness, she has emptied her home of the people she cares about and become a broken vessel that can't hold the love her own husband tries to send. If she could have started the past year again, she would have read to Nell and taken her into the garden every day instead of bringing basket after basket of vegetables to soldiers at the Walker home. She would have never met Jed, never given birth to a child that she couldn't keep, never sent Cassie away, never raised a daughter who wanted to be with Cassie more than with her. Going back further, she would have stopped the South's secession and the bitter war that kept Edwin from her and his only child.

As Amanda reaches the iron fence at the cemetery entrance, she dabs her eyes with a handkerchief. She walks silently past boards standing vertically in the ground, marking new graves of soldiers. Nothing grows in the recently dislocated red dirt, not even weeds. A raw wind gusts up from the James River, which borders one boundary of the cemetery. The water looks pewter colored, wearing down the rocks as it flows around craggy Belle Isle, where captured Union soldiers are imprisoned.

Nell's grave is in a quiet section bordered by holly trees. Amanda stands before it, swaying, crossing her arms and cupping one elbow with each hand.

"Nell," she whispers. "Nell, can you hear me? I wish you were still next to me but I hope you found my Mummy and she's teaching you some new rhymes."

Amanda closes her eyes and hears the wind carry echoes of hundreds of women like her, reciting whatever words can comfort them beside the graves of those they have lost. The wind chills the tears on her cheeks as she kisses the top of the cross on Nell's grave, then begins the long walk home.

CHAPTER THIRTY-SEVEN

Cassie walks Jacob up and down the stable, pointing out each horse and talking in a low voice.

"White mane, black nose. Brown spots, black tail," she says. Jacob simply blinks. She sighs, then keeps talking. It's easier to pace up and down between the stalls than to sit quietly in the tack room or in the sleeping loft.

The door scrapes and she moves back into a corner, cowering until she knows whether it's safe to come out. She hears Clancy's plodding gait, followed by steps that sound swifter. She cautiously walks towards the sounds, edging along the doors to the stalls.

A boy's reedy body blocks the light from the door. He swings his long arms, throwing shadows onto the hay. Cassie peers up at him. His coffee-colored skin looks like her own, but his forehead furrows above a flat nose and full lips that look more like Clancy.

"Gabriel?"

"Yes."

"Hello," says Cassie.

"You know me?"

"From when you was a little boy. I been watching over you." He crosses his arms.

"You feeling well?"

"Yes."

"Helping your daddy?"

"Yes."

"You used to be little as this baby," says Cassie, holding up Jacob.

Gabriel shrugs and shifts his weight from one foot to the other.

Cassie wants to rush to him and run her hands down his

arms, his face, his back, just to remind herself of his solidness. All these years, she has remembered him more like a sketch than a painting with all the colors filled in. She is not sure she would recognize him except for his dark eyes, always alert and over-sized.

"Sit a spell," she says, motioning to the hay bale next to the chair in the tack room.

Gabriel looks at Clancy for permission. Clancy stands by the wall, hat in his hand, and says, "All right. A little bit now. Then back to Master Pete."

Cassie goes to the corner of the room, dips water from a bucket into a tin cup, and places it in front of him. She also dips a cup for herself. Then she pulls out a piece of cornbread that Julia brought her for lunch, breaks it, and hands him half. She sits with Jacob propped against her shoulder. As Gabriel eats, she watches what seems like the miracle of his jaws moving as he chews and swallows, then sips the water. She wants to memorize each movement he makes, and each utterance, however terse.

"Julia, she a good cook," Cassie says.

"How you know Julia?"

"I know both of you from a long time ago," says Cassie. "Long ago."

He shrugs again.

"How you getting along?"

He wrinkles his forehead. "All right, I reckon."

"You like horses like your daddy do?"

"Yes." He looks at Clancy and stands up.

"Master Pete, he gonna ask for me."

"May the good Lord bless you, Gabriel. I be watching over you, too."

Gabriel smiles then, brightening the room as if his teeth were a row of candles.

"Goodbye, then," he says, and he turns and opens the door. Clancy motions that he will come back later.

"Goodbye, son," she says, but he's already out the door.

Cassie peers through a crack in the boards of the stable wall as Gabriel walks down the lane to the carriage house. His bare feet kick up puffs of reddish dust. She watches until she can see nothing but the puffs blowing in the early March breeze.

CHAPTER THIRTY-EIGHT

Returning from the cemetery, Amanda rounds the corner from 26th Street to East Grace and notices a movement on her front porch. From this angle, all she can see is the gray sleeve of a Confederate soldier's uniform. Composing herself for the news that Edwin is dead, she straightens her dress. She looks the part, already wearing black.

After she opens the gate, it takes her a few seconds to recognize Edwin standing before her, scuffing his muddy boots on the doormat. His shoulders seem too large for his gaunt body. A full, chestnut-colored beard streaked with wiry strands of gray hides most of his face. The bright sun shows grime-filled lines on the back of his neck. A bandage winds around his head, covering his right eye. Inside a deep hollow, his left eye looks like a tea stain on a tablecloth.

He reaches out to her and pulls her into one long, wordless embrace. Concern washes away all her carefully rehearsed scenes of how she would greet him if he ever did come back. She sags against him, overwhelmed by his presence. He's dirt-smudged, reeking of sweat and unwashed clothing, but still upright.

They stand on the front porch, holding each other, swaying. Finally Edwin pulls back and says with a smile, "Can a man come into his own home?"

Amanda leads the way through the front hall. Edwin props his rifle, muzzle up, behind the door. His heavy haversack clunks down near the bottom of the stairs.

"Why the black dress?"

Amanda takes in a breath so big it hurts her chest, then lets it out slowly.

"You didn't get my telegram?"

"What telegram?"

"Oh, Edwin. I don't know how to tell you this." Her voice

breaks. "We lost...we lost Nell." She begins sobbing, her face in her hands.

Edwin staggers into the parlor and then turns back to Amanda.

"What was it? Measles? Smallpox? Pleurisy?"

"No. Worse than that. She ran into the street and a carriage hit her."

Edwin takes an awkward step back and collapses on the sofa.

"When?"

"Just about a week ago."

"Our little Nell," he says, his voice trailing off. He clenches his hands together tightly.

"I thought you knew," says Amanda.

Edwin's face has gone white.

Amanda sinks down onto the sofa next to him.

"I never meant...it was so dreadful...," she says.

Edwin slouches and presses his palm against his good eye.

Finally, Amanda looks up and says, "Let me get you something to drink and heat some water so you can wash up. What happened to your eye?"

"Where's Cassie?"

"She ran off. A lot of slaves in Richmond have run off."

"When? Why didn't you send news of it?"

"I was going to. But then with all that happened to Nell, I just couldn't...I just didn't..."

"Did she run away after Nell's accident?"

"No, no, nothing like that."

"I thought Cassie was trustworthy," says Edwin tightly.

The heels of his boots dig into the carpet. He places his hat on the cushion next to him, revealing matted hair that loops over his ears. Amanda wonders when he last sat on an upholstered seat—and when someone cut his hair.

Amanda runs her hands along the bodice of her dress, hoping her body doesn't sag too much underneath.

"But what about you? Your eye is all bandaged. It must be serious if they sent you home."

"I was in no shape to fight at Waynesboro," he says, then points to his face. "That's from a minie ball I never saw coming. Good thing it didn't do much more damage. It shattered my cheekbone but the doctor thinks my eye will heal."

"And you've come home to bad news," says Amanda.

"I'm going back, as soon as I'm able. The colonel and my men—"

"Don't think about all that. Wash up and let me make you something to eat. It won't be much. Times are lean."

Edwin leans back, unbuttons his jacket, and closes his eye.

In the kitchen, Amanda ladles out water and places it on the stove. She wishes she had made a better breakfast. All that's left over from the morning is a half-eaten bowl of rice mixed with dried apples. The heartiest food she can make right away is potatoes with carrots. She climbs down the ladder to the root cellar and brings up a basketful of vegetables to clean, cut up, and boil.

When Amanda goes back into the living room, Edwin is smoking his pipe. The tobacco reddens and crackles as he inhales.

"The water is hot. Come out and wash now," she says. "I'll get a basin and towel."

Edwin removes his jacket and goes out to the back steps so he won't splash onto the kitchen floor. Amanda pours water over his hands and hands him a bar of soap. The lather turns gray, then black, before she pours rinse water over his outstretched hands. He had such soft hands when they first married. Most of the time, he worked at his desk or went down to supervise the loading and unloading of tobacco barrels. Hired men did the heavy warehouse work. Now the backs of his hands are chapped and cracked, the nails chipped. She has no salve to rub into them.

She wets a cloth and hands it to him so he can scrub his neck and beard. When he's finished, he towels off and hungrily sweeps her with his eye.

"Help me upstairs," he says. "Lunch can wait."

Amanda hesitates. It feels too soon to join him in bed. It would be easier in the dark, when she wouldn't have to worry that he would notice the purplish marks of her pregnancy with Jacob, scrawling out the evidence of her treachery. How can his lust overpower everything—his injury, his hunger for a hot meal, his shock over Nell's death?

"There is so much sadness right now," she says, trying to stall.

"We mustn't dwell on sadness," he insists. "I have seen so much sadness in my time away. So much loss. But desolation is unhealthy. For so long, every day, I've thought about coming home to my wife and her tender comforts."

He holds out his arms and she steps into his embrace. It would be heartless to deny him right now. She turns and leads the way through the house, climbing the stairs slowly, his footsteps behind her.

In their room, she returns his kiss lightly at first. Then she opens her mouth and their tongues probe each other greedily. As she peels off her dress and underpinnings, he touches her too eagerly to notice any evidence of her recent pregnancy. His hands feel thicker, rougher than Jed's, but she forces herself to banish the memory of Jed's delicate caresses. In this overheated rejoining with Edwin, she feels rushed and desperate. She wants his seed to wash out remnants of Jed and their baby, somehow purifying her.

CHAPTER THIRTY-NINE

After it grows dark, Julia returns to the stable, bringing dinner for Cassie wrapped in a square of cloth. Clancy lit the lantern before he left "for the quarters," as he put it, but Cassie knows he is going to see Molly. Julia lowers herself onto a bale of hay and settles her daughter while Cassie bites into a ham biscuit, then smiles.

"No ham to be found in Richmond right now."

"What's it like there?"

"More people than you ever seen. All manner of colored and white, all thronged together in the streets. So many wagons and carts. So many soldiers. Dust and commotion."

"You like it?"

Cassie chews and watches Julia. Her daughter's once chubby cheeks have elongated into planes that the lantern light flattens even more. Her body has stretched out and filled in to the point where Cassie would likely not recognize her on the street anymore. Only the birthmark on the side of her neck, a jagged streak of dark skin about the size of Cassie's pinky finger, looks familiar.

"The Carter folks in Richmond treat me better than the Scruggses. But you and Gabriel, I never stop thinking about you."

While Cassie eats the second biscuit, Julia says, "Mama? You going back there?"

"I aim to drop off this baby with his aunt in North Carolina."

Julia walks to the door and back again. In the next room, a horse whinnies and paws.

"I want to go with you."

"You and your baby?"

"Yes, us both. I can be wet nurse to that white baby until

you drop him off. I still got my milk. No more bottles and begging folks for cow's milk."

Cassie bites her bottom lip. It's risky to begin traveling with a runaway and a second baby. There are dogs and patrollers everywhere. The patrollers would sell her, even sell the white baby right out from her arms. Julia and her baby could be sold, too, or chained and roughed up before being returned to Master Scruggs. Worse, she and Julia could once again be forced to separate.

"I come back for you. Then we go where we want. Maybe up north where there ain't no slaves."

"No, Mama. I can't watch you leave again. Take us."

Cassie shakes her head.

"Don't leave me here again," begs Julia, her voice cracking.

"Never want to leave you the first time."

"Take me now. Me and Katie."

"You reckon your daddy will come?"

"No. He got his other young'uns. Besides, Master let him do what he want because Master loves them horses so much."

"Master Scruggs get a notion, he sell Clancy faster than a horse."

Julia puts her arms around Cassie.

"Don't go, Mama. Don't go without me," she repeats, then sobs into Cassie's chest. Julia's tears slowly dissolve Cassie's hesitation. There's no telling what they will encounter, but it could not be much worse than having to separate again. She has already lost any hope of reconnection with Gabriel.

The door to the stable swings open with a loud creak and in walks Clancy. He hands Cassie an apple, then says in a low voice, "You leaving?"

"With Julia and Katie."

Clancy sets down his lantern, sits on the broken chair, and sucks his teeth.

"Who got the notion?" he asks.

"I did, Papa," says Julia.

"How you aim to travel?"

"Stagecoach," says Cassie. "With money and the pass."

"The pass, that be for you and the baby. Not for two extras, both val-u-a-ble property of Master Robert Scruggs," says Clancy, exaggerating his speech to sound like a slave owner.

"Could change the pass."

Clancy rubs his hands on his thighs. "Need a white person for that."

"Let me walk up to the big house—through the front door—and ask Missus Scruggs," says Cassie.

"Ooh, my, I have seen an app-pa-ri-tion," Julia says, clapping her hand to her forehead and swooning to imitate the mistress. "This looks like my Cas-sie, but I sold her away long ago. Julia, bring me my smelling salts di-rect-ly!"

When they stop laughing, Clancy says, "Hear talk of a Methodist preacher up by Gravelly Run. He help runaways. What you have to do is knock on the door and say, 'Reverend Branson, please, could you lead me in prayer?'"

"You ever meet him?" says Julia.

"No. I hear talk. He supposed to help folks is all I know."

Julia says, "Mama, you got to take the baby to that family? His own mama don't want him. Leave him up at the Scruggses'. Let them worry what to do with him. Like as not, they take him in. Then we just leave and go north."

Cassie picks up Jacob and rocks him.

"I ain't giving Master Scruggs nothing. Why give them a new baby to turn mean-spirited? This baby, he need a good home. His mama never give me trouble. Sure, she kind of foolish, but she never beat me or say I steal from her. She love this baby and want him to grow up with his daddy's people instead of strangers. Ought to do right by her."

"Who more important, her or us?" says Clancy.

"I want to do right by this here baby," says Cassie.

"Might end up worse off than you is now. Way worse," says Clancy.

"Nothing worse than being sold away from your young'uns," says Cassie in a flat voice.

"And you about to go and leave me," says Clancy to Julia. "You and my only grandbaby."

He walks over and touches Julia's shoulder. She leans against him. The lantern casts their shadows on the wall, a mural of two heads almost indistinguishable from each other.

"I grew up without a mama," says Julia quietly.

"And Gabriel, he have a new mama," says Cassie.

Jacob begins fussing and Cassie hands him to Julia. She sits on a bale of hay and opens her dress to nurse him. Cassie watches Jacob root around, then latch on to the nipple, unconcerned about giving up his bottle and having a new person feed him. Julia is right. Letting her nurse Jacob will make traveling much easier.

"Before we go, I got to know something," says Cassie. "Who Katie's daddy? He gonna follow us or tell stories about where to look?"

Julia and Clancy say nothing.

"He white?"

Julia nods.

"Master Scruggs? He make his way around the quarters, all right. Guess I was too much up in Missus Scruggs's face all day for him to bother with me."

"The younger one. Bobby."

"The one who got himself killed?"

Julia nods. "Missus Scruggs has a notion about it. She no fool."

"What choice you have?"

"He was kind to me."

"Got what he wanted."

"I got his only child. Now he dead and gone."

"And he ain't gonna come looking for you."

Clancy sits quietly, rubbing his hands together. Finally, he says, "Well, if you bound and determined to go, let's think on a way to get y'all over to Gravelly Run. No time to waste."

After Julia goes back up to the Scruggs house with Katie, Clancy and Cassie climb into the loft. Once Jacob is settled, they lie stiffly next to each other, not touching, but not sleeping.

Finally, Clancy says, "You on a fool's errand."

"I ain't giving up now."

"Come back for Julia."

"What difference do it make if she run now or she run later? We gonna stay together."

Clancy sighs.

"Come with us."

Clancy sighs again and rolls away.

"I ain't surprised. You still got Gabriel. He don't even know me. And Molly."

After a few moments, he turns towards Cassie and opens his arms to her. "Rest up now. You gonna be doing some hard traveling."

She curls against his chest and cries for the family she used to have.

While it's still dark outside, Clancy wakes Cassie. Julia has quietly walked down from the big house with a sleepy Katie and a bundle of extra clothes and food.

There's a half moon, but enough light for Clancy to lead the way down a path to the lower pasture. Spikes of wet grass look silver next to their feet. Cassie wishes she could reverse time to the summer nights when she and Clancy would steal away from their separate sleeping quarters, stifling their giggles, their desire to lie together speeding their footsteps. Now he walks quietly, efficiently, barely turning back to look at her and Julia.

Clancy stops at the fence and points the way to the reverend's house. "Just through those woods and up the hill. Nobody here know Julia gone yet. Walk fast as you can."

"How to thank you?" says Cassie, balancing Jacob with one arm and curving the other around Clancy's stiff shoulders. She tilts her face up to kiss him, but his lips barely pucker. Tears underline his eyes.

"Get gone, woman. And quick. I don't want no trouble," he says, blinking. Then he turns and hurries back up to the stable.

The stars fade into the lightening sky as they make their way down the edge of a newly plowed field, skirting a corncrib and a smokehouse. Each woman carries a baby and a bag. When Jacob begins to cry, Cassie thrusts her thumb into his mouth to quiet him.

After Cassie knocks on the door of the reverend's house, she hears rustling. Then a voice calls through, "Please state your business."

"Reverend, please, sir," Cassie says, her voice trembling, "could you lead us in prayer?"

CHAPTER FORTY

As Edwin walks into Nell's bedroom, Amanda nervously follows. She hasn't yet disturbed anything. The doll lies face up on the pink and white quilt, as if Nell will soon return to lift her and brush her hair. Amanda thinks that putting anything of Nell's into a sack makes it all too final, as if Nell had never existed. It's bad enough to be left with no trace of Jacob except the empty cradle and a small blanket she carefully tucked under a pile of sheets in the hall linen closet.

Edwin looks around, rubbing his beard. He takes in the hairclips and ribbons on the bureau, and the pitcher and washbasin, each half filled with water. A small dress hangs on the back of the door. His knees buckle and he thuds down on the bed. Amanda sits next to him, rubbing his back, her guilt an ember in her chest.

Finally, he sits up straight and says, "Pack the clothes and bring them up to the Female Orphan Asylum, where they can be put to good use. It pains me too much to see these things."

"But what will we remember her by?"

"Sometimes it's better to remember nothing when you have lost so much."

Amanda stands up. "I didn't even think…I should have cut a lock of her hair. I just couldn't bear to look after… after…"

Edwin reties the sash on his purple dressing gown, a relic from the days when Cassie served them hot coffee and fresh rolls each morning. The cloth billows around his diminished body.

"A lock of hair will not bring her back. You need to get this home back in order. It's repugnant that you have to take on the tasks that a slave should do."

"But Cassie…"

He waves his hand dismissively. "What use is there in finding someone to look for a runaway now? Take the money I set

159

aside before the war and hire someone."

Amanda swallows, her throat dry. "I can manage for now."

"Can you? The house looks deserted, like nobody is tending it properly. Find a colored woman who is free to be hired out. What has become of Reverend and Mrs. Walker? Maybe they can send one of their servants our way for a time."

"I haven't seen much of them lately," she admits.

"But don't the men at her wayside still need your help?"

"Gardening season is just beginning."

"Surely you can do more than grow vegetables for them."

"I haven't felt up to it."

"You must force yourself away from this desolation," he says. "Nothing good will come of it. This I know from bitter experience."

He leaves the room, his footsteps thudding down the hallway. She walks out and pulls the door shut before following him to their bedroom. When he reaches for her, she feels stiff but she turns to him anyway, playing the part of the dutiful wife.

Later, she wakes to the unfamiliar gurgle of his breathing. She lies still, the darkness so dense that she can't even see her hand in front of her face. Feeling her way, she gets up, pulls the chamber pot from under the bed, and squats over it to piss, no longer embarrassed by that when she has so much more to hide.

When the room lightens enough for her to see her way to the door, she tiptoes down the hall to Nell's room. She sits on the side of the bed and strokes Nell's pillow, releasing a faint trace of the girl's light pine odor. Edwin wants her to return this room to starkness, but Amanda lies down and pulls Nell's blanket over her shoulders. The warmth circles her like Nell's thin arms, holding fast, forgiving.

CHAPTER FORTY-ONE

The door to the parsonage swings open, and a bent man with white eyebrows sticking out like hay from a rack ushers them inside. Though the first streaks of sun brighten the sky, thick curtains dim the main room. A fire sputters in the hearth, and a stout, white-haired woman in a shawl stirs something that smells like cornmeal mush in a cast-iron pot held up by a fireplace crane. She waddles over and kneels while the reverend leads the Lord's Prayer.

After "Amen" reverberates across the room's bare wood floor, the reverend softly asks if they have anything else they wish to pray about. Cassie understands this as the invitation to explain their situation.

"Reverend, sir, I pray for the health of these two babies. I carry a white baby to North Carolina for a family to adopt him. This here wet nurse and her baby come with us." She pauses to nod at Julia. "I got a pass. She don't," Cassie continues, trying to hint that Julia is a runaway without actually saying so. She hands the reverend her pass. He glances at it, still on his knees, and says, "I see."

He adds, "Jesus said, '*I am the light of the world: he that followeth me shall not walk in darkness, but shall have the light of life.*'"

Then he stands and motions Cassie and Julia to do the same. The woman heads back to the hearth.

"Do you need shelter here?"

Cassie considers this question. How much should she trust him? He and his wife seem kind, but they could be tricking them.

"Well, maybe, for a time."

"First, you must see the safe room. You may sleep there. And if anyone knocks on the door or approaches the house, this is where you must go without delay," he says.

He walks to the hearth, where his wife lights a candle and hands it to him. Cassie and Julia follow, each holding a baby. He moves to the back of the room and lifts a cassock from a peg on the wall, revealing a doorway that only comes as high as Cassie's shoulder. He opens the door and crouches, leading the way down five steps to a dirt-floored passage. Two pallets and a chamber pot line the left side. Cassie wonders who has stayed here before, and for how long. Light comes through the cracks in what seems to be a door on the other side.

"This leads to the church," he says. "You should be safe inside here, but do your best to hush those babies. They could give you away." He leads the way back upstairs. "Now, are you hungry?"

Missus Branson sets the table and then returns to the pot.

Cassie and Julia eye each other. They don't expect to sit at the table where the white folks usually sit.

Cassie remains standing and says, "It ain't proper to sit there. Y'all have a kitchen table out back?"

"No, no," says Reverend Branson, motioning to the table. "Sit here."

Missus Branson spoons out a portion of mush onto each of four plates, then passes a jug of syrup. It is the first time Cassie has ever sat at a table with white folks and eaten off the same kind of plates that they do. She lifts each spoonful cautiously, worried about spilling or somehow offending the Bransons. Julia keeps her head down as she eats, then excuses herself to nurse the babies.

Once her plate is empty, Cassie isn't sure what to say. Never before has a white person served her. Cassie decides to say thank you. Missus Branson holds up her hands, palms forward, and shakes her head so vigorously that a lock of white hair falls across her eyes. "Not at all," she says. "You need all the help we can give you."

After Julia returns to the table, Reverend Branson asks,

"North Carolina, you say? Whereabouts?"

"Town called Little Washington, where the Tar River meets the Pamlico," says Cassie, repeating what Amanda told her.

He nods, takes his hat from a peg beside the door, and goes out. Cassie wonders whether he is going to give them away to a slave catcher. Her eyes feel grainy with fatigue, but she forces herself to be stay up and be watchful. She also wants to somehow repay Missus Branson for her kindness. "You got any mending?"

Missus Branson gets up and brings in a sewing basket and an apron with a hole in the pocket. "I'd be pleased for your help."

"And let me cook you something," says Julia.

Missus Branson laughs. "With what, plaster in the walls?"

"Have you more cornmeal?"

"A little."

"Well, that will do for cornbread," she says, standing.

Missus Branson glances around the room. Katie sleeps on a folded blanket in the corner. "I'll hold this baby. He's so sweet tempered," the old woman says, reaching for Jacob, clucking and cooing.

Cassie pokes the needle into the apron's worn cloth and pulls the thread through. Missus Branson's eyes look the same blue color as Missus Carter's. On a day like today, Missus might be folded into the corner of the parlor sofa, her face pale as milk above her beloved book of verses, one arm around Nell but her lap empty of Jacob. Cassie silently prays that Amanda will find the strength to pay enough attention to Nell, and also to begin turning the soil for new rows of beans and tomatoes.

Reverend Branson returns, scraping his muddy shoes on a mat before coming into the main room. He sits on the edge of the sofa and speaks quietly.

"The way to North Carolina could be dangerous for the four of you," he says. "The less I know about where you came from, the safer you will be. But I ask you to tell me the God's honest truth. Will a master be looking for any of you?"

"Me," Julia whispers. "And my baby."

"I see," says the reverend, clasping his hands together, bringing them up to his mouth, then dropping them again. "But you are all heading south together, not north?"

"Yes, sir," says Cassie.

"And how soon might someone be looking for you?"

"Soon as they figure out I gone," says Julia.

"Do they have any place they might look first?"

"Richmond, maybe. Got my...," Cassie begins.

"Whoa, there. Don't tell me what I don't need to know. But that's good. That's in the opposite direction of North Carolina."

He nods at Cassie. "Let me see your pass again."

When Cassie hands it over, he reads it carefully and then gives it to Missus Branson. The two go over to the hearth and confer in low voices. When Missus Branson returns, she looks closely at Julia.

"What name do you go by?" she says.

Cassie looks sharply at Julia.

"Hattie," says Julia.

"Come over here, next to the window," says Missus Branson, leading the way. Reverend Branson stands next to her.

Julia gives Cassie a worried look but follows. Missus Branson pulls the edge of the curtain back so the daylight falls on Julia's arms and face. Reverend Branson puts on his spectacles and peers intently at Julia's hand.

"Uncover your hair. Let's see what it looks like," says Missus Branson.

Julia unties her scarf to reveal a tidy part in the center of her head. She has coiled her flat, black hair into a bun at the back of her neck.

"Thank you," Missus Branson said. She lowers the curtain and tells Julia to wait there while she and Reverend Branson speak privately again.

When they go to the hearth, Cassie comes over to Julia and whispers, "What they up to?"

"They look me all up and down like they gonna sell me to the fancy trade."

Cassie cringes. "Why they feed us and let us sit at their table like we white folks if they aim to sell us?"

Reverend Branson returns with Missus Branson following.

"We think you'll pass," he says.

"My pass? You got my pass," says Cassie.

"No. We're going to dress Hattie as a white woman with two babies. You're going to be her maid."

"But she…"

Julia widens her eyes to silence her mother.

"What I got to do?" Julia says.

"First of all, don't talk. Even if you have a gift for impersonations, you may not sound exactly like a white person, especially if you get nervous. Missus Branson will find some clothes for you. Keep your head covered and wear your gloves. Your hands might look a little too dusky. I can find a trusted friend to put you on the stagecoach down to North Carolina on Friday. After you drop off the baby, find some Yankees in blue uniforms and you tell them you want protection. They're all over East Carolina. If you stay with them, you'll be free from slave catchers. You're going to have to cook or do other work, but you won't have a master."

Missus Branson picks up the pass and says, "Just in case something goes wrong, I'll add in the name Hattie and her baby girl. But if all goes well, you shouldn't have to show it."

Reverend Branson says, "Let us pray now for God's protection." He kneels and motions for Cassie, Julia, and Missus Branson to do the same.

Cassie looks down at the worn wooden planks in the floor and thinks it could use a good sweeping and wet mop. One day, she vows, she, Julia, and Katie will have their own home to keep clean. "Amen," she says.

CHAPTER FORTY-TWO

Amanda brings a washbasin into the parlor and tells Edwin it's time to change his bandage. The doctor who examined him at the field hospital near Waynesboro advised that Edwin keep his eye covered, changing the bandage once a day, to give it a better chance of healing and having his sight fully restored.

Edwin sets his pipe and ashtray on the top of his desk. His head aches. Sitting upright seems to help, so Amanda has set a pillow in the desk chair. He rests his legs on a stool and wears the uniform jacket that Amanda washed and mended. His warehouse has little business right now, as enemy troop movements have made roads treacherous for wagons. Most trains that used to carry tobacco barrels have been requisitioned for the war effort. Barrels of tobacco are stacked to the rafters, waiting for transportation.

When Amanda unwraps the bandage and gently touches him with a damp washcloth, he draws in his breath and grasps her elbow. Uncovered, the side of Edwin's face looks like a ferocious animal took a bite from it. His eye is still swollen shut and his cheek sags over the shattered bone. One cheek will always be flatter than the other, even when he heals, but a full beard will hide most of that disfigurement. His injured eye now looks more sunken than swollen, though the flesh around it still looks irritated and pinkish liquid seeps from it.

"Steady, now. In a minute, I'll be done," she says. "You're being brave."

"Is this what you said to all those men who passed through Mrs. Walker's wayside?"

"I don't remember what I said. I helped them however I could." She unrolls a clean bandage. "You had another nightmare last night," she says.

"I don't recollect."

"You shouted in your sleep. You kept saying, 'To the rear! To the rear!' I tried to wake you but I couldn't."

Edwin grimaces.

"What were you talking about?"

Eyes still closed, Edwin shakes his head.

"I reckon you're bothered by something," says Amanda, tying the bandage around his head.

"No point in telling it. Nothing can bring him back."

"Bring who back?"

Edwin opens his good eye. A tear springs out and rolls into his beard. "I told you, there's no point. For all these months, I have seen such losses. Terrible, sanguinary losses. But I have vowed to myself not to succumb to remembrance. It would make me too desolate. I need to be able to go out again and do my duty."

"But maybe owning up to it will help you end these nightmares."

Edwin begins to smack his right fist into his left palm.

"Jones. Rum, they called him. That was his nickname from West Point. He had a fondness for the drink all right, but he was intelligent and brave. I was supposed to protect him and help him rally the brigade..."

"Go on," says Amanda gently.

"He was on his horse right in front of me. I saw...I saw...oh, it's not fit for your ears. I tried to make it up to him in the Mule Shoe, but the men behaved like curs. All they did was run out and surrender. I should have been captured, too. Or killed, for all I was worth in getting them to follow orders. And then..."

"Oh, Edwin, maybe it wasn't your fault."

"Not my fault? An officer died because of me. How can I put that out of my mind? Are you able to put Nell out of your mind?"

Amanda gasps. "No. Of course not."

"Why did she run across the street?"

"Because she thought...she thought..." Amanda can't finish the sentence. She can't even stay in the room any longer. Though it's a blustery day and the herbs are nothing but nubs poking up through the red dirt, she wants to feel the rush of air across her face, snatching away the truth.

CHAPTER FORTY-THREE

Four days after Cassie and Julia arrive at Reverend Branson's, a Quaker farmer with a wagon brings them back to Petersburg to catch the stagecoach. Julia, disguised in a hoop skirt, rides up front next to him. Cassie sits in back with the babies. Missus Branson wrapped a scarf around Julia's neck and jaw and added a frilly bonnet with a brim wide and floppy enough to cover most of her face. The wraps go along with the story that Julia has a toothache and it pains her to talk. Cassie, playing the part of servant and nanny to two babies, will answer questions for Julia, who now goes by the name of Missus Harrison.

Cassie and Julia's stagecoach journey from Petersburg passes in thumps, bounces, and snatches of scenery. There's early fog in fields bordered by tangled vines, stands of maples and oaks jumbled with buds. Sun bears down on green ground cover, jolt after jolt on the plank road. As they move south, hardwoods give way to mostly pines. Then there's mud, thick under the wheels, which makes the horses strain.

A white woman in a dress decorated with fraying green ribbons and a slave girl who looks about twelve years old climb on at Belfield. The woman introduces herself as Missus Franklin and asks Julia where she is going. Julia looks distressed and points to the scarf around her neck, so Cassie answers.

"I don't know why on earth anyone would go east of Greenville," says Missus Franklin. "Haven't you heard tell that Little Washington is in ruins? The Yankees burned it down and sent all the slaves away. Thank goodness it's in Confederate hands again."

"Harrumph," says Julia. "Damned Yankees."

Cassie glares at her.

At a midday stop to switch the teams of horses, Cassie steps down and walks around to ease the stiffness in her back while

Julia goes into the front room of the tavern, puts a blanket around herself, and nurses each baby. A new driver comes and tells Cassie and Lettie, Missus Franklin's slave girl, to go to the back door of the building for something to eat. They sit at the kitchen table and sip steaming mugs of broth. After the drafty stagecoach, the warmth of the room makes Cassie drowsy and she closes her eyes.

The driver comes back and growls, "Wake up, you lazy niggers. Time to go!"

Cassie startles. She expects to see a young Julia sitting on the floor and playing with her rag doll in the room they share with Clancy.

"Yes, sir," she says, remembering where she is.

Julia sashays down the front porch, holding both babies. She seems to be enjoying her new role as a Missus. She coughs, nods at Cassie, and holds out the babies for Cassie to take from her. The white gloves cover her hands.

Back in the coach, Julia's head droops and nods. Cassie gazes across the seat at her daughter and remembers rubbing Julia's face with a wet rag, wiping away dirt and sweat until her light brown skin shone. Now Julia's daughter rests under one of Cassie's arms, and Jacob under the other. The motion of the coach soothes both babies so they spend most of their time sleeping.

At the stagecoach inn in Tarboro, Cassie arranges for overnight lodging, explaining that her owner is too plagued by a toothache to talk. When they close the door to the room, Julia strips off the scarf and gloves and sits on the bed, the hoop skirt tilting into her face.

"Cassie, I told you, I want supper di-rect-ly! Fetch me some hot water. I am fa-tigued from my travel!"

Cassie chuckles. "Better not get too high and mighty. Someone knock you right back down soon as they look too close at your face."

Julia unbuttons the dress and begins nursing Jacob.

"No wonder white ladies always fainting. They wear too many clothes."

"I never slept up in a real bed before," says Cassie. "Hope I don't roll off."

"I shall sleep up here, while you shall sleep with the babies. Do not let them dis-turb me!" says Julia.

In her mimicry, Julia sounds like an exaggerated version of Missus Scruggs. It's entertaining, but Cassie knows if she's trying to pass, she needs to make her voice sound less shrill and more like a white person might really speak.

Cassie says, "You ain't got the sound quite right. Say that again. I gonna close my eyes and see if I hear a white person or my Julia trying to sound white. Don't want no one figuring you out."

Julia repeats the sentence.

"You got to work on the endings. Say everything real clear. Sleep-p-p!" says Cassie, popping the p.

"You shall sleep-p-p with the babies," repeats Julia through pinched lips. She raises her shoulders, sniffs haughtily, and then starts giggling.

"Why surely, Missus," says Cassie, playing along. "The floor my natural home."

They both laugh, then fold up blankets and place them on the floor to make beds for the babies.

Before bed, Cassie kneels and thanks Jesus for helping her reunite with Julia, then asks for protection for the rest of the journey. She surveys the room for any sign of what might happen next, but it's too dark even to see her hands folded in front of her nose. When she climbs into the bed, she falls asleep next to her daughter's warmth, cosseted by the unfamiliar softness of cotton sheets and feather pillows.

CHAPTER FORTY-FOUR

In the garden in Richmond, mouse-colored clouds flit across the horizon. The wind brings the murky scent of the river. Amanda paces between the withered debris she has yet to clear from last year's vegetable rows. Edwin is growing suspicious about Nell's accident and she has to put an end to it. If only she had back-tracked to Nell's side that day instead of letting the girl lag behind her. If only Nell had not spotted someone who looked like Cassie. If only...

Amanda stops herself and picks up a spade. Gardening will keep her from having to talk to Edwin. She pulls out the old plants, turns the soil, and sprinkles in a bit of wood ash. Returning to the kitchen, she carries out the spindly pea plants from the windowsill—the ones she planted with Nell. Her back aches as she digs holes, turning her foot sideways to measure the width between each one. After she sets each plant in its hole, she gently props up the pea tendrils on a trellis.

These plants started when Nell's fingers pushed the seeds into the soil and sprinkled dirt over them. Each orb the size of Nell's thumbnail germinated and sent forth green shoots. The plants will flower soon, and then pods the shape of an eyebrow will slowly descend and fatten. These peas will one day feed Amanda and Edwin, but not Nell.

Amanda pauses, then propels herself upstairs to Nell's room and carries out the washbasin and pitcher. She blinks as the tears come, but that doesn't stop her from lifting the washbasin and pouring the water that once rinsed Nell's face and hands over the seedlings.

"May these plants grow big and strong for you," says Amanda.

Next she goes to the corner of the garden and chooses a stem from a camellia bush. Using shears, she carefully makes a slanted cut behind a leaf node. She carries the cutting to Nell's half-filled pitcher of water and places the end into it. Later, she will put the cutting into a shallow container of soil, and mist it often by lightly flicking water over it with her fingers. It could take until June for the cutting to root, but when the new camellia is strong enough to survive in the garden, she will find a special spot to plant it.

Finishing as the first thick drops of rain begin to thud into the garden makes Amanda feel light, as if she's one of those balloons used for surveillance in the war. Yet thoughts of Jacob chase away her remembrance of Nell. There is still no word from the Spencers.

It's lunchtime, so Amanda washes up and sets a skillet on the stove. She managed to buy bacon at the J.S. Robertson grocery but isn't quite sure how to cook it. Supplies have been so scarce that Cassie never had a chance to show her what to do. Amanda puts a wad of bacon in the pan and hopes for the best.

The bacon hisses. Amanda pokes it with a fork. It looks mushy, not crisp. Drops of grease singe the insides of her wrists. She winces and dabs at herself with her apron.

Though the bacon curls into a greasy pile, she sets the table and calls Edwin into the dining room. They eat silently, forks clinking against the dishes.

CHAPTER FORTY-FIVE

At the stagecoach inn, Cassie goes downstairs to get breakfast, saying it's for her Missus. She returns to the room with a plate of grits and gravy and a mug of something that's supposed to be coffee but smells more like shoe leather.

Julia says, "I'm gonna lick the china for them white folks and make it extra dirty."

"You gonna still pretend you white after we leave Jacob?"

"The longer I act white, the more folks let us move around and not ask questions."

"What if someone find out you ain't white? Then we in a heap of trouble."

Julia hands Cassie the plate and spoon and tells her to finish the grits.

"Well, I best be white for today," she says.

"Wish I could decide what color to be."

"It ain't easy to keep quiet and to cover yourself up."

"Yeah, but you get to go first. Walk like you own the sidewalk. Get to be yes ma'am-ed by the driver and all the folks at the inn. Sit and fan yourself, let us clean up after you. You a fine lady! How you like it?"

Julia picks up the corset. "Cassie? I need help with my toilette! Hurry! I must look pre-sent-able when I go out."

"Best not get too used to it," says Cassie.

The second stagecoach follows the Tar River east to Little Washington. Along the way, the land flattens and pine trees grow thick along the banks. The water bristles with logs and other barriers set up to keep Union ships from moving through.

A half an hour after they leave, Cassie hears the pounding of hooves and pulls back the curtain. A Confederate lieutenant rides up and orders the driver to halt.

Julia's eyes become stirred up as a wash pot. Cassie nods her head slightly at Julia, then sits up straight and clasps her hands more tightly around Jacob's back.

Missus Franklin says, "What on earth is the holdup? We don't have all day. My mother and father are waiting for me. They said it's not safe for me to stay in Belfield anymore without the protection of my husband, may he rest in peace." She sniffs and pushes loose strands of her straw-colored hair back up into her bonnet.

The soldier dismounts and holds his rifle across his body. The jacket and pants of his hand-sewn uniform are mismatched shades of gray. A black beard billows out from his chin like a thundercloud. "Who are you carrying?" he demands.

"Women and children," says the driver.

The soldier yanks open the curtain.

"Niggers and babies is more like it," he says, looking at Cassie and Lettie. Then he notices Julia and the white woman. "Oh, pardon me, ladies."

Missus Franklin scowls.

"Give me something to eat," he orders Cassie.

"Here, sir," says Cassie, reaching into the basket that Missus Branson packed for them and handing him an apple.

"Lay it on the seat," he says so he won't have to touch her hand, then grabs it and takes a bite, spattering juice on Cassie.

"Why are you traveling?"

Julia sneezes and coughs, so Cassie answers.

"Missus Harrison right here, I look after her babies." She points to Katie, whose face is nestled against Julia's shoulder. Then she lifts Jacob so he faces the officer, showing off Jacob's slate-gray eyes and reddish hair to prove that he is white. "We on the way to her kin. Ain't safe for us up Petersburg way."

Missus Franklin identifies herself and says she and her slave girl are on their way to her parents' home in Winterville.

The soldier looks around again, hand on his rifle.

"What are you hiding in there?"

"Why, nothing!" says the white woman.

"Step out," says the soldier, cocking his head. "I need to see for myself."

"Lordy, this trip is already taking a coon's age," she says, gathering up her skirt and giving her arm to the soldier so he can help her climb down.

The driver stands beside his horses, one wiry arm looped through the reins. Sprigs of gray hair poke out underneath his straw hat. He looks at his watch and spits into the weeds.

The passengers stand behind the stagecoach as the soldier climbs inside and rummages around. He steps back out, chewing on a roll from Missus Branson's lunch basket. With his free hand, he motions to Cassie and Lettie.

"Come with me," he orders. Cassie begins to sweat. She hands Jacob to Julia and brushes a finger across her lips when Julia tries to speak.

"This is highly improper," says Missus Franklin.

"We have orders to search all darkies between Goldsboro and Greenville for secret messages. There's some kind of Yankee spy plot afoot and we need to snuff it out," he says.

Cassie trudges slowly towards a stand of pines, the rifle butt prodding her shoulder. She tries to let out each breath slowly to calm herself, but she ends up panting.

"Now, then," the soldier says once the stagecoach is out of view. "Both of you, dresses off."

"But...," Lettie protests.

"I said, dresses off!"

Cassie unties her rope belt, pulls her shoulders out of the neckline of the dress, then lets the fabric slide around her ankles. Blubbering, Lettie gets tangled up in the dress as she tries to pull it over her head. When Cassie steps over to help, the soldier yanks the dress hard enough for it to tear and flings it down. A stream of piss wets Lettie's left leg.

"Worse than pigs," he mutters, then commands, "Arms up.

That's right. Over your head. Now, walk in a circle."

He draws two X's in the dirt with the tip of his boot and tells each one to sit on the X. Despite the warm day, Cassie shivers, circling her knees with her arms. As they watch, he pats Lettie's dress, searching for papers. When he picks up Cassie's dress, Cassie hears her heart thudding in her ears. She gave Julia the Confederate bills, but a gold piece is still hidden in the hem of the dress.

"I just an old nigger baby nurse. Please, sir, you know I ain't got nothing," Cassie says.

"What's this?" he says, holding up the pass.

"A pass to travel, sir. Permission of my Missus."

"Ain't your Missus sitting right next to you in the coach?"

"She ain't my main Missus. She the daughter."

"How do I know you're not a Yankee spy toting a secret message?"

"Sir, I ain't no spy. Paper tell you all you need to know about me."

"The paper says nothing now," he says, ripping it into bits so small that they blow away like ashes.

Cassie swallows around the lump that clogs her throat. Lettie squirms and sniffles. The soldier leers at Lettie's smooth, shiny skin and budding breasts.

"You're a pretty little thing," he says, reaching for her shoulder. Lettie crosses her arms against her breasts. "Lie down."

Lettie sprawls face down in the dirt. The soldier unbuttons his pants. Cassie looks away.

The beat of hurried footsteps interrupts the soldier just as he pries open the girl's legs with his knee. Another soldier makes his way under the trees, pushing boughs out of his way. His cheeks are red, his cap askew.

"Quit piddling around, Baylor," he tells the first soldier. "We've got to move out."

"Aww," says Baylor. "Me and these darkies were just getting

acquainted."

The other soldier frowns. "Put your clothes back on," he orders Cassie and Lettie, "and stop wasting time."

The two soldiers march Cassie and Lettie back to the stagecoach. Before they can climb aboard, a wagon train thunders through in a staccato of horse hooves. Dust drifts over the canvas covers of each Confederate wagon, obscuring the artillery and rations inside. Cassie covers her mouth with her hand, but particles drift in anyway, dry and bitter.

"What an impertinent soldier," says Missus Franklin after they climb back aboard, eyeing Lettie's disheveled dress. "He didn't...oh, he didn't..."

"No'm," says Lettie, sniffling and rummaging through her tote sack for a rag to wipe her nose.

Julia readjusts her gloves as she searches Cassie's tight face. Cassie presses her lips together and lowers her head. Instead of reaching for Jacob, she puts her palms together and beseeches the Lord not to forsake her as the stagecoach jolts along the flat, swampy terrain.

CHAPTER FORTY-SIX

Edwin lies on his uninjured side, his bandaged forehead jutting out from the sheet. One hand, fingernails still dirty despite daily scrubbings with a brush and warm water, rests next to his face. It's March 10, the day that President Jefferson Davis has set aside throughout the Confederacy for fasting, humiliation, and prayer. Churches will be holding services and staying open throughout the day. After dressing quietly, Amanda lightly pulls the covers over Edwin's shoulders and walks out.

The dawn air looks Confederate gray as Amanda passes St. John's Church. It's a long walk down the hill and past the capitol to Reverend Walker's church on the west side of Capitol Square, but she wants to hear the pastor who comforted her after Nell's death. The other Richmonders out walking this early nod solemnly at her, then hurry along.

Amanda slips beneath an arched entry into the sanctuary and sits at the end of the pew, one of many women dressed in black. The reverend flaps his thin arms to welcome all. He reads from President Davis's proclamation: "*It is our solemn duty, at all times, and more especially in a season of public trial and adversity, to acknowledge our dependence on His mercy, and to bow in humble submission before His footstool confessing our manifold sins, supplicating His gracious pardon, imploring His divine help, and devoutly rendering thanks for the many and great blessings which He has vouchsafed to us.*"

Though President Davis is talking about the adversities of life in the Confederacy, Amanda imagines herself at the base of God's footstool, a solid, polished mahogany block that towers above her shoulders. There, she silently confesses her own manifold sins and begs for divine forgiveness. Does Jesus really forgive the adulteress and the mother whose two children are lost to her?

When Reverend Walker leads an unfamiliar hymn, she tries

to picture Jacob in the doughy arms of Mrs. Spencer. By now, Cassie should be on her way back to Richmond. Amanda has checked the post office nearly every day for word from North Carolina, only to be rebuffed.

Her worries preoccupy her so much that she barely hears the rest of the service. When she walks back out to the street, the brightness of the cool but sunny morning temporarily stupefies her. How did she end up on this street corner in Richmond, twenty-two years old, living in a home with an iron fence in front and a brick wall in back, a garden overrun with vegetables instead of flowers, an injured and preoccupied husband, a daughter killed in an accident, and a secret son, now missing? Maybe it's just as well her own parents died so young and did not have to witness her shame.

When Amanda stumbles into the post office, the clerk smiles and hands her a letter with Mrs. Spencer's name on the return address. This must be the news that Jacob has arrived and Cassie is on her way back home. Joyfully, Amanda rushes back outside, tears open the envelope, and leans against the stucco wall of the building while she reads.

> *March 3, 1865*
> *Dear Mrs. Carter,*
> *I hesitate to write you this letter but I want you to know that we are still waiting for your package to arrive. We were prepared to receive it more than one week ago and we cannot understand the delay, even with the road conditions being poor due to spring rains and over-use by soldiers, supply wagons, caissons, &c. We have everything prepared and pray the traveler who accompanies the package is having a safe passage. I will send word as soon as it arrives.*
> *Yours sincerely,*
> *Mrs. A.A. Spencer*

Amanda's face sags. Her long feet feel like clods of dirt, but she forces herself to walk into the grounds of Capitol Square. The memory of Jacob's small weight in her arms threatens to topple her.

She inhales sharply and gazes up at a bronze statue of George Washington mounted on a horse, his right arm raised in a gesture of command. How resplendent he looks, how confident in the future of his new nation. Could he have envisioned his native Virginia as part of a different country, some of its finest military men buried, Richmond's grand streets now overcrowded with soldiers and pompous politicians from all over the South? Suddenly she feels tired, so tired that she can't believe her skeleton still supports her body. Everything has failed to live up to its promise.

Amanda walks along Franklin Street, back up Church Hill, deliberating. For a block, she imagines keeping her secret, letting Cassie and Jacob simply vanish. She could become pregnant with Edwin's child and start a new household. Edwin would never need to know.

Yet after she crosses Shockoe Creek, she imagines the relief of confessing everything to Edwin in a wild tumble of words. The idea of pretending to be a dutiful wife for the rest of their days together, knowing she will never live up to his memory of dear departed Mildred, seems unendurable. Banishing herself to the Sisters of Charity will be the punishment she deserves. She quickens her pace, heart and feet thumping together. A cool breeze undercuts the buds. As she climbs the stairs next to Mrs. Walker's house, the words of John 8:32 clang in her head: *"And ye shall know the truth, and the truth shall make you free."*

CHAPTER FORTY-SEVEN

The stagecoach inn in Greenville smells of the cabbage that must be cooking for supper. Cassie lies back on the bed and closes her eyes. Does Jesus walk with her or has he turned his back? Faces of the people she has recently seen rotate in her head. Missus Carter, pale and tear-stricken, handing over the baby. Sulking Gabriel. Clancy carefully turning his hat brim around and around. Blood whooshes in her ears and her breath feels strained.

Julia has stripped off the dress and hoop. Wearing a chemise and petticoat, she settles both babies on the bed and paces. Afternoon light outlines the edges of the closed shutters.

"Mama, when can we go?" Julia says.

"Not so fast," says Cassie, eyes still closed. "We ain't got the pass. We both runaways now."

Julia pulls off the petticoat. "You think they looking for me?"

"Master Scruggs? Sure of it. But you still have the white lady clothes," says Cassie. "They ain't looking for no white lady."

"And your Missus? She looking for you?" asks Julia.

Cassie opens her eyes and sits up.

"She be mighty troubled once she find out her baby ain't where he supposed to be. No telling what she do."

"Why don't we take him to the family where he supposed to go and then keep going?"

"Maybe Missus have someone there waiting for me, take me back to Richmond, take you back to Master Scruggs."

"Let's stay here for now, then."

Cassie presses her hands together. Baylor's face whirls in front of her, his breath rancid, his leer revealing teeth sharp and yellow as a rat's. Men like him must be marching around everywhere, ready for an excuse to torment colored women.

"That ain't gonna work forever. Real white people, they

nosy. They like to get up in your face and ask, 'Who your people? Why you here? Where you going?'"

Julia says, "I make up whatever answer they want to hear."

Cassie shakes her head. "The money Missus give me bound to run out, sooner or later. We got to find them Yankee soldiers soon as we can. Best chance we have to be safe."

"And baby Jacob?"

"He best off with us for the time being. Who we gonna ask to take in a little baby, even if he white? Folks ask too many questions."

"I already look like a white lady. What you gonna do to hide yourself?" says Julia.

Cassie rubs a corner of the bedsheet between her thumb and forefinger while she considers this. "Got me a needle and thread in the satchel. Let's make me a mammy apron. We go out, people see a white lady, her young'uns, and a mammy. You got a better idea?"

"Ideas hurt my little ol' head," jokes Julia, batting her eyelashes.

"Enough of that fool white lady act," snaps Cassie. "Hand me the bag. Time to get to work."

In the satchel, Cassie pulls out one of the baby blankets. It's a bit dirty but it will do for an apron.

"Get on over here and help," she directs Julia.

While Julia stretches the blanket tight, Cassie tears off a long strip from the bottom. From that, she fashions two strings, then sews them to the sides of the blanket. Next she hems the bottom of the blanket to hide where she tore the fabric. She stands up and tries it on, circling in front of the crack of light at the shutters, the effect like a strobe.

Julia blinks. "You too thin," she says.

Cassie rummages in the bag, pulls out Julia's slave dress, and stuffs it into her bosom.

"How you going to hide your face?"

Cassie looks through the bag again. She needs a big, white head wrap.

"Your scarf," she tells Julia. "You ain't got no toothache no more. You got to talk this time. I gonna be the fool."

After wrapping the scarf around her head, taking care to cover her forehead to just above her eyes, Cassie stands up once again and twirls in front of the door.

"What you call yourself?" says Julia.

"Hattie."

"Why, Hattie, my ba-by is fil-thy! Get right over here and clean her up," says Julia in her imperious voice.

"Guess this will do," says Cassie. "Hope nobody look too close."

"We got to go through town?"

Cassie nods. "You hear that white lady, Missus Franklin, talk about Yankees across the Tar River bridge? We going there."

"How we gonna get across? I saw secesh soldiers on guard."

"Gotta think up some kind of story. You already say you make up whatever the white folks want to hear."

"When can we go?" Julia asks again.

"Rest now and think on what we gonna say. We go towards dark in case we got to hide in the woods on the way."

Julia sighs. "Mighty hard to rest when all I want to do is move on."

"We close, now. So close. Got to pray for patience," says Cassie. She pulls the Bible from the bag. "Missus Spencer don't need this. Put your hand on it and talk to the Lord."

CHAPTER FORTY-EIGHT

Amanda returns to Edwin's pipe smoke clouding the air in the entrance hall. She pauses, then walks resolutely into the alcove and places the letter from Mrs. Spencer on the desktop next to Edwin's ashtray.

Before he can ask her about the prayer service, she blurts, "I have received some disturbing news. I have not wished to burden you, but now I feel you must know."

As Amanda talks, Edwin puts down the pipe and rests the un-bandaged part of his forehead against his hand. He keeps his gaze on the floor as she ends with Cassie and Jacob's departure on the train, and Mrs. Spencer's letter saying that they have still not arrived.

"I was foolish and impetuous. If I could take everything back, I would. I beg for your forgiveness," she says.

He remains silent, his head still in his hand. She walks through the dining room into the kitchen, then looks out the back window. The daffodils nod. She returns to him. He has not moved and refuses to look at her or speak.

"I am unworthy of you," she finally says, and walks out of the room.

Upstairs, Amanda surveys the bedroom for anything she should take with her when she knocks at the gate of the Sisters. The lacy counterpane on the bed, the silk dress from her first year of marriage—that can stay. All she wants are two extra dresses, a shawl and a cloak, the sketch that Jed made, the pink and white baby blanket that Aunt Margaret sent to Nell, and the tiny one that Jacob used. From the upper bureau drawer, she takes her mother's gold locket with her father's picture in it, one of the few things her parents passed down to her. She can sell it if necessary. That and her wedding ring. Cassie took their only satchel, so Amanda pulls the top sheet from the bed and wraps everything into a bundle.

In the silent house, she can smell Edwin's pipe. Walking out the back door into the garden, she sets down her bundle and surveys the peas. Their delicate tendrils wrap around the bottom of the trellis. She hopes it rains enough for them to grow tall. Along the wall, she stops at the edge of the compost pile and sinks down to her knees. The earth feels warm beneath her. She curls up on her side and lets the smell of rich, steaming decay surround her, as it already surrounds Nell. Closing her eyes, she tries to still her cartwheeling thoughts.

Amanda wakes to silence and darkness. Behind the magnolia tree, the house's roof makes a dark point among the stars. She'll leave at first light when the Sisters are more likely to answer her knock. If she identifies herself as a destitute war widow, no one will know where she came from and what she did.

CHAPTER FORTY-NINE

Julia cracks the stagecoach inn door open and peers out. All looks quiet. She has donned her disguise again and walks carefully, the hoop swaying around her. She keeps Jacob in her arms while Cassie holds Katie. Most of Katie's face is now hidden under a frilly bonnet that Cassie made from the bottom of a petticoat.

They walk around the edge of the boggy field to avoid the main streets in the town, moving as swiftly as possible while keeping to the road's edges. Paving made of oyster shells crunches. When Cassie hears wheels coming towards them, she motions Julia into a stand of pines. Cassie waits, breathing hard behind a tree trunk. A farm wagon loaded with jugs of milk, driven by an elderly white man, passes. Cassie lets out her breath. Since it's near the end of the day, they encounter no one else on foot. As the road widens, they hear hoofbeats again. They scurry off the road once more and watch two soldiers in gray coats ride past on skeletal horses.

The town looks eerie in the graying light. The bridge looms ahead, a dark line over shining water.

As they approach, the Confederate soldier on picket yells, "Halt!"

Cassie's sweat soaks the inside of her white head wrap. She rocks Katie back and forth, playing up the mammy role.

"Shh, baby girl," she says when Katie whimpers.

The soldier comes close enough for her to see his whiskers bristling like a field of wheat. There's liquor on his breath.

"What business have you on the other side?" he says, addressing Julia.

"My ba-by," Julia says slowly, carefully. "She has a powerful toothache. We need to see a doc-tor."

"Where?"

Cassie thinks quickly, remembering what Missus Franklin said about where her parents live, and forces herself to giggle foolishly. "Oh, Lordy! It have a funny name. Win...twin... something-ville."

"Winterville?"

"Why, yes, sir!" says Cassie, holding Katie close to her chest. "That where we going, right, Missus?"

Julia nods.

The soldier comes close to Julia.

"Wait here. A lady and her babies can't cross alone."

He goes and wakes another soldier to take over the picket, then returns to escort them. Rough wooden planks laid cross-ways make up the bridge. To one side, the debris juts out of the water. The soldier dilly-dallies, making the most of the chance to do something besides march back and forth with his rifle on his shoulder. Cassie watches her toes, willing herself to stay one pace behind the soldier when all she wants to do is rush away from him and his stinking breath.

"So tell me, ma'am," he says to Julia, smiling flirtatiously. "Whereabouts is your husband? Is he serving?"

Cassie tenses, hoping Julia will be brief.

Without hesitating, Julia answers, enunciating clearly. "He was killed at Gettysburg. These ba-bies are his only children."

"I'm sorry, ma'am," the soldier says, nodding at Julia. "Many fine men have been lost in this war."

Julia twists her face into a pained look, rocks Jacob back and forth, and nods.

When they finally reach the other side, the soldier says, "Go right to the doctor's home, ma'am. Yankees are all through here, especially further south. You need someone to escort you?"

"Why, no thank you," says Julia.

Katie begins to cry. She's wrapped tightly in a blanket and wants to move around.

Cassie forces another giggle. "We sure gonna hurry with

this here baby girl fussing like she do!"

"Good night and thank you kind-ly," says Julia. She walks steadily ahead, moving south of the bridge, her back straight, her bonnet like a sail. The setting sun spills what looks like gallons of peach-colored paint across the flat horizon.

As soon as they are out of earshot of the soldiers, Cassie re-arranges her white turban to wipe the sweat from her forehead and exhales. Julia lightly brushes her mother's arm with her gloved hand.

Winterville proves to be little more than a cluster of farms. Afraid to stop there, they keep walking, giving Katie a dry biscuit to chew to keep her occupied. Jacob sleeps. Cassie and Julia say little to each other, hoping to pass through as quietly and quickly as possible.

As they pause in a stand of trees for Julia to nurse the ba-bies, Julia whispers, "You aim to walk all night?"

"If we have to," says Cassie.

Julia whispers, "Never thought I'd come this far from Mas-ter Scruggs."

"And more to go," Cassie answers, "Lord willing."

Chapter Fifty

Stepping onto the back porch, Amanda hears no movement from Edwin. The inky air is beginning to wash with light. Dew from sprouting weeds brushes her bare ankles, but the day should warm as soon as the sun rises. Once she gathers a bit of food, she will walk down to the Sisters, ready to give up her identity as Mrs. Carter, wife of a Confederate soldier and prosperous Richmond tobacco merchant. She plans to begin calling herself Mrs. Edward, using her father's first name as her last name. If anyone asks for details, she'll say her husband died at Spotsylvania Court House and she has no children and no family members left.

Though food seems unappetizing, she needs to fortify herself if she's going to be leaving home. The pot of cornmeal mush she made yesterday morning still sits on the stove. Standing, eating straight from the pot, she gags on the thick mixture but manages to swallow three spoonsful. A cup of tea will help. She goes out to the well, brings water into the kitchen, and builds up the fire.

The least Edwin deserves is a kind goodbye note. Since her own writing paper is in her lap desk upstairs, she goes to Edwin's desk in the alcove and pulls out a sheet of Carter Tobacco stationery and a pen. She sits at the kitchen table, writes "Dearest Edwin," then stops to think about exactly what to say.

The water has started to boil when she hears Edwin's feet thumping down the stairs. Though she is tempted to dash out the door, she wills herself to get up and stand in front of the stove.

He wears the baggy, knee-length shirt that he slept in and walks barefoot. The skin around his good eye sags and so do his broad shoulders.

"Why?" he says in a voice so soft she wonders if she heard

him. Then he repeats his question.

She puts a lid on the pot of water, moves it off the heat, and turns to face him.

"There's no good reason. With you gone, I was lonesome. So lonesome. You didn't write to me for such a long interval. I didn't know…I thought…"

He squeezes his hands together. "I am away defending our country and I am as good as dead to you?"

"I said there's no good reason."

"You have dishonored me."

"I know I am no longer worthy of you. That's why I'm leaving."

"Where do you aim to go?"

"I'll find a place."

"But in this city, with Yankees massing about nearby? It's dangerous for a woman alone."

"I reckon I don't have much more to lose."

Edwin sits in the kitchen chair, his hand on his forehead. He pushes the sheet of paper to the edge of the table.

"What were you planning to write?"

"That I'm sorry. So dreadfully sorry. And you should go to your brother and his wife. They will take proper care of you."

She turns to get her bundle. Tea right now is out of the question. Her stomach and throat feel tight.

"Do you love him?" Edwin asks.

Amanda clasps her hands together and looks down. "He was charming. He courted me."

"But do you love him?"

"I thought I did. But I was just carried away."

"Are you going back to him?"

"No. He has a wife and boys."

Edwin places both palms on the table. "I was better off in the army."

"You never loved me anyway."

"What?" he says, jerking his head up and then wincing at the pain that the sudden movement causes.

"I'll never be what your first wife was to you."

Edwin shakes his head. "Amanda, how could you misunderstand things so completely?"

Amanda covers her mouth with her hand.

Edwin continues, "I remember the day I rode over to borrow that wagon and saw you all grown up just like it was yesterday. I thought I couldn't possibly want to marry again after all I went through with Mildred. But there you were, your head high, smiling as you brought an armload of flowers from the garden. You looked so fresh, so energetic, not at all fragile and in need of constant care. It took my breath."

"But she was so beautiful."

"She was sickly and…well, no matter. She is gone. When I saw you in that field, I had some hope that I would be able to find happiness again."

"And I ruined it all," Amanda says. "Edwin, I wish I could undo everything. You deserve better."

She blinks so she can see her way out. Pulling the back door closed behind her, she walks toward the gate. Sage and mint sprout at the edge of the rows she planned to fill with beans, tomatoes, and cucumbers. The rusty hinges in the gate grind open. She steps into the alley, walks to the end, and turns the corner.

Grace Street is still quiet at this hour, with the early morning sun slanting against the iron fences in front of each house, creating long shadows. The steeple of St. John's Church glows a pale yellow as she makes her way along the street before turning down to East Franklin. How many times did she walk this way with Nell? The bundle of her belongings makes her gait unsteady, so she switches it to the other side.

When she reaches the brick wall below the churchyard, she sets the bundle down and looks around for a passing carriage. She listens for the clop of horse hooves and hears nothing but the crunch of approaching footsteps. Looking up, she sees a gray uniform, then the white bandage around a man's right eye.

A breeze stirs the loose dirt and pollen in the street.

Edwin reaches her side, panting to catch his breath.

Amanda feels hope surge into her chest, but it's too much, like taking a swig of brandy after years of teetotaling. Her head feels like it might float off her neck.

"I need you," he murmurs, his voice ragged.

She reaches out her hand to him and he takes it.

CHAPTER FIFTY-ONE

Cassie peers through pine needles at three men in dark coats with long rows of buttons that gleam in the rising three-quarter moon. She is relieved to see military clothes instead of the plain pants and shirts that slave catchers might wear. These coats look different from Confederate uniforms, and the caps look flat on top. Maybe they belong to some kind of home guard.

After the men pass, Cassie steps out for a better look. The cloth is dark blue, not gray, though the moonlight might be playing tricks on her. She goes back under the trees and sends Julia out.

"Think they Yankees?" Cassie whispers after Julia returns, even though no one seems to be around to overhear them.

"I can't tell," Julia whispers back. Katie has fallen asleep on Julia's shoulder, her breathing heavy, her arms splayed around her mother's chest.

They step back onto the road. Cassie holds Jacob. Her legs feel leaden but she wills herself to continue. Moonlight turns the pine trees dark gray with jagged edges. Yet the road shines bright as water, tapering to a V shape in the distance. Cassie feels like she's floating, pulled along by a powerful current.

After more than an hour, the road curves slightly and Cassie sees white triangles of tents rising from a field. Scattered around, fires glow in bright splotches. When she gets closer, Cassie smells coffee, a heady aroma that sends her back to earlier times, when she ran the Scruggses' kitchen and Clancy could stop in whenever he took a break from the horses. A soldier stands and stretches. His frock coat hangs to his mid-thigh. It looks like the coats worn by the men that passed on horseback.

"Missus Harrison," Cassie says to Julia. "I do believe we done found them damned Yankees."

"Have we?" says Julia in her white lady voice. "Well, I de-clare! This must be our luck-y day!"

When they get even closer, Cassie whispers, "Time for you to turn colored again."

Ducking into a stand of trees, Julia steps out of the hoop and the petticoats. After Cassie helps Julia take off her corset and bonnet, Julia exhales loudly. Her face, like tea with milk, is exposed once again. Cassie takes Julia's slave dress out of her bosom and hands it over. Julia slips it on and kicks away the hoop, where it lies like a beached boat.

With a smile that fills the lower half of her face, Julia picks up Katie and says, "Ready, Mama?"

Cassie swallows, trying to moisten her dry mouth, and nods.

Julia starts running, carrying Katie. Cassie follows, barely registering the weight of Jacob in her arms, her white mammy headscarf a pale comet against the moonlit sky.

CHAPTER FIFTY-TWO

In Hollywood Cemetery, Amanda arranges a bouquet of wild bluebells on Nell's grave while Edwin places his hat over his heart. It's the first Sunday in April. Bells from St. John's and other churches reverberate into the cloudless sky.

Though headaches still occasionally plague Edwin, he can now open his injured eye for a few minutes at a time to discern outlines and large shapes. He has replaced the bandage with an eye patch that Amanda fashioned from a piece of black fabric and a ribbon, her stitches crooked but serviceable. Last week, he sent word to the War Department that he's ready to serve again. Since he's good with figures, he expects to be assigned to help the quartermaster with accounts instead of fighting in the field.

"Goodbye, sweet Nell," says Amanda, kneeling in front of the headstone and brushing the dirt off her fingers. "We'll visit again soon."

Edwin nods, then returns his hat to his head. Amanda reaches up and rubs Edwin's neck. He turns and places an arm around her shoulder. The mild air feels like a tonic. Since their reconciliation, they step lightly around each other. Several days before, they carefully folded and packed Nell's belongings to donate to the Female Orphan Asylum. When they finished, all they saved was the pink and white baby quilt that Aunt Margaret sent, carefully wrapped around Nell's doll and hairbrush. They both kissed the bundle and Amanda took it to the hall closet. As she opened the door, she pulled out Jacob's baby blanket and held it up to her nose. No scent of him remained. She kissed that, too, and imagined the blanket as a sail on a boat that brought Jacob safely to his new home. Then she made herself shut the door with a click.

Today, Amanda says, "It's such a fine day, let's walk a ways. Do you feel up to it?"

"The headache has held off so far. It will do me good."

As they make their way past the Monroe Square military grounds, they see people strolling serenely to church, the warmth easing their tight shoulders. Amanda looks up at the spires and crowns of trees that stand tall above the city's dusty sprawl. Near Capitol Square, she is surprised to see hordes of people rushing past. Inside the capitol grounds, a barrel-chested man practically knocks her over.

"Watch your step," Edwin shouts after him. Amanda wonders why everyone is in such a hurry. They haven't heard the cannons or guns that might indicate that the city is under siege.

A man carrying a heavy trunk stumbles on an uneven spot in the path, sets the trunk down, and wipes his brow with a handkerchief. He asks a gray-whiskered gentleman in a dark frock coat if he can lend a hand.

"Yes, but may I inquire first, why is everyone hurrying so?" asks the gentleman.

"Haven't you heard? General Lee has sent a telegram to the War Department," says the sweating man, his face splotched and his hands flying up like startled birds. "The news is not good."

"Do go on," says the gentleman.

"Well," says the sweating man, his voice lowering. "I'm a clerk at the Treasurer's Office. I hear tell that the lines at Petersburg have broken. The government is to evacuate Richmond as soon as possible."

"Evacuate?" the gentleman repeats. "Petersburg has fallen?"

"Oh, indeed it has," says the other man.

"Help us, O God," says the gentleman.

"Right now, help me with this trunk. Sir, I beg you to pick up that end. Hurry!"

Amanda feels like a flattened bellows. The cloudless sky, now merciless as a sheet of ice, mocks her exuberance about the fine day.

Edwin stops walking, his body rigid. "I must present myself

to the War Department right away."

"But you haven't been reassigned yet."

"I will ask for an immediate assignment. It's an emergency!"

"But the dangers..."

He buttons his jacket, then takes her hand between both of his and squeezes it tightly. "First, you need a place to shelter. If the Yankee ruffians surge into the city, you must not be home alone."

By the Custom House, a group of men gathers around a pile of papers on fire. Other men are rushing out of the building with Confederate government documents, handing them over to be burned. People laden with baggage head down the hill to the James River and Mayo's Landing. Amanda overhears a man saying that the Danville railroad line still runs and will be the fastest way out of the city. Clusters of Richmonders chatter excitedly. Some bid each other goodbye.

They pass two women in straw bonnets who together struggle to carry a large ham. They have come from the crowd outside a commissary with its doors flung open. Other people straggle out, loaded with bags of coffee and barrels of flour and sugar. The sight of such bounty hidden away by profiteers when supplies were so scarce at the markets angers Amanda. The crowd of greedy people surges around her, elbowing each other and shouting, threatening to knock her down.

On Franklin and Eighth Streets, Edwin points to Reverend Walker's church. Its thick stone walls are likely to withstand whatever siege comes. The commotion fades as they step inside and close the door behind them. At the altar, Reverend Walker talks quietly with a group that has gathered around him.

Edwin briskly approaches. Amanda lags behind him, ashamed of herself for only coming to church once since Nell died.

"Reverend, good afternoon," says Edwin. "We come to you in haste, as I feel sure you have heard the terrible news. I need to inquire for the sake of my wife, is it safe to stay here?"

"As safe as it will be anywhere in Richmond at such a time."

The reverend peers over Edwin's shoulder. "Mrs. Carter. It's been some time since we have seen you."

Amanda nods. "You were so kind to me when I lost my daughter. I just...I felt.... Now, I am sorry to return to you in another time of crisis."

Mrs. Walker strides up in a mauve silk dress with white bows sewn around the wide skirt. On her neck she wears a gold locket. Her cheeks flush like petals of Lenten roses.

"Well, what a surprise to see you among us," she says. Her frosty eyes sweep across Amanda's waist. "Why haven't you come back to help me once again? Even though it's not yet vegetable season, the men are certainly in need of someone to comfort them."

Mrs. Walker purses her lips. Amanda clenches her sweaty hands.

"With my husband home..."

"Of course," Mrs. Walker says, eyes narrowing. "We must have a word later." Then she closes her eyes and draws her hands together. "For now, let us pray for the safety of the children and all the citizens of Richmond. If we are to be captured, we must not let our enemies see us so wretched and in despair."

"Please take good care of my wife," says Edwin. "While I defend our city."

"We must pray for you, too," says Mrs. Walker. Then she walks up onto the altar and seats herself on a chair. She opens her Bible and begins reading in a calm, sonorous voice. *"Fret not thyself because of evildoers, neither be thou envious against the workers of iniquity. For they shall soon be cut down like the grass, and wither as the green herb."*

Amanda accompanies Edwin back up the aisle to the door, taking slow, measured footsteps. The more she hurries, the sooner he will expose himself to the enemy. A desperate, makeshift command will take charge of defending Richmond and he will be at their mercy. Her eyes tingle in the dim entrance hall.

"I wish you wouldn't…"

"I know, but I cannot stand idle. Let us not prolong this goodbye. You know that I will return to you as soon as I am able."

"Let it be soon," says Amanda. "And let me be the wife you deserve."

Edwin gathers her in his arms, the top button of his jacket pressing into her forehead. She pushes her weight into him, as if her body could leave an imprint. All too soon, he releases her, opens the door, then hurries into the reckless crowd roaming and shouting outside.

CHAPTER FIFTY-THREE

When a Union sentry calls out, "Halt!" Cassie and Julia both stop. The light from his lantern distorts his eyebrows into caterpillars.

"Halt right there," he repeats, his voice booming from beneath a blue cap. A second sentry points a rifle at them.

The first soldier circles, holding up the lantern. His nostrils twitch.

"Hoo-eee! It seems we've got us some reeking contraband. Keep 'em covered," he says to the second soldier. "I got to go find Robinson."

Cassie looks up at the moon. It doesn't look much bigger than the lantern, but it's a powerful beacon hung by God himself. Julia wraps Katie tightly in her arms. Cassie feels the moonlight spilling across her forehead, anointing her.

Robinson clomps over in heavy boots, cap askew, mouth scrunched.

"What the hell you want this time of night?"

"Please, sir, we just two poor slaves with two young'uns. We give ourselves up to your protection," says Cassie, her voice steady.

Robinson's spit lands an inch from Julia's foot. Julia steps back, shifting Katie from one hip to the other.

"Sit down," says Robinson, pointing with the barrel of his rifle to the patch of dirt right where he spat.

Cassie wants to sink to her knees and pray for mercy from Robinson, from God, from anyone who will listen. Instead, she lowers herself onto her backside. The sentry still points his rifle at their heads. Cassie resettles Jacob, who nestles his head against her neck. The heat of his small body makes her skin clammy. Julia sits next to her mother, crossing her outstretched legs at the ankles, balancing Katie on her lap. Cassie notices that

Julia breathes hard, eyes like a horse about to bolt. Insects whirl in the lantern's circle of light.

"Where do you come from?" he asks.

"Up Belfield way," says Cassie quickly so Julia won't jump in with something closer to the truth.

"Do you know how to do laundry?" he asks. He pronounces the word like "lan-dree" in a voice that sounds like it comes through his nose.

Cassie wants to laugh. She expected questions about whether they ran away and whether a master is looking for them.

"Yes, sir," she answers. "We done plenty of laundry in our time."

"Good. We need workers here, not lazy niggers loafing around," he says, then turns and walks away.

"Go wake Dix to replace you on the picket and bring 'em to the rear!" he shouts to the first soldier.

Cassie and Julia continue to wait on the damp ground until the first soldier returns. He motions them up and they follow his bobbing lantern through the camp. The second soldier brings up the rear, his gun now pointed down. Many soldiers sleep on the ground, wrapped in blankets, rifles lying next to them. The long metal barrels glint in the firelight. One group sits around a fire, passing a bottle. Their high-pitched laughter sounds to Cassie like horses whinnying.

At last, they reach an area with makeshift tents patched together from sheets, shirts, and rope.

"Contraband camp is here," says Robinson, waving an arm towards the area.

"Thank you, sir. Please, we need water," says Cassie.

"I've helped you out enough. Ask one of these niggers laying about."

"Everybody asleep, sir," says Cassie.

"I have no orders to take care of you stinking people," he says, then pivots on his heel and leaves.

Cassie sits on the ground and motions for Julia to do the same. Julia holds Katie in her lap. The grass is damp with dew. Cassie grimaces, pulls out her cloak, and spreads it on the ground for them to lie on. Her shawl and mammy apron will have to do as blankets. They lick the grass for water.

Cassie huddles on the cloak and pulls her shawl over her shoulders. She settles Jacob near her head so she can keep an eye on him. The pit toilet must be nearby, as foul odors spiral through the dark.

"Freedom sure do smell sweet," says Julia.

Cassie chuckles. Then Julia starts laughing, more and more loudly until they both laugh so hard that they writhe on the ground and have to gasp for breath. Jacob whimpers and Katie stares at them in wide-eyed confusion. A stranger in the camp pokes his head out from underneath a dirty blanket and tells them to hush up. Cassie wipes her eyes on the mammy apron, whispers a quick prayer of thanks, then falls asleep with one arm around Julia and the other around Katie.

CHAPTER FIFTY-FOUR

Throughout the rest of the afternoon, Amanda shelters in a pew near about two dozen congregants. Reverend Walker has barred the doors, but they still hear a near constant creak and rattle of wagons, carriages, pushcarts and conveyances of all kinds carrying fleeing Richmonders. Reverend Walker brings stale biscuits and wine from his study, divides them up and passes them around.

An elderly man offers to slip through the back gate of the churchyard and do a brief reconnaissance on the streets outside. When he comes back in, he locks the door behind him and limps into the sanctuary.

"It's utter pandemonium," he says. "Someone smashed barrels of whiskey to keep them out of enemy hands. Beastly sots are scavenging from the gutter. There is looting and pillaging everywhere. Men and women plunder one thing, then throw it into the street to take something they like better."

Reverend Walker shakes his head and says, *"For what is a man profited, if he shall gain the whole world, and lose his own soul?"*

Some of the ladies at the front of the church sing "God Save the South." In the evening, Amanda pulls a cushion from one of the pews and puts it on the floor by the wall. Worries about Edwin keep her from resting. He's almost certainly caught up in the chaos. Most of the others in the church are lying down, so she walks to the back of the sanctuary and lets herself into the churchyard. Its tiny garden should be safe from the melee and the Yankee soldiers, whenever they come. She hopes to find solace by walking along the tidy border of boxwoods, but the air is pungent with the fermented odor of whiskey. Ashes blow like snowflakes, stinging her eyes. A fire must have started down towards the river. Streaks of light thread the clouds. The sky, roiled by flames, looks bright as day.

Richmond seems to be ending in an apocalypse. Confederate soldiers are trying to destroy anything valuable that the enemy might take, and they seem to be taking down the entire city instead. Amanda kneels under a flowering dogwood tree. Dew on the grass soaks through her dress. If ever there is a time to pray, it's now. She closes her eyes and asks Jesus to protect Edwin and to watch over Jacob, wherever he ended up. A memory of Cassie among the tomatoes, filling basket after basket, handling each tomato like a jewel, jolts her. Maybe Cassie didn't abandon Jacob and run away, but something else detained her. Mercy washes through Amanda, easing her tense neck. Now Amanda says a prayer for Cassie, too. Instead of hearing the wind rush, Amanda feels like a strong, warm hand is pressing between her shoulder blades.

She is still kneeling when a loud blast stuns her. The concussion knocks her flat. She claws at the grass before another blast comes. The garden trembles beneath her. Glass tinkles behind her as one of the church windows blows out. Pushing herself up, she makes her way shakily to the side door and stumbles back inside. Reverend Walker stands on the altar with broken glass sprayed around his ankles.

"We must leave!" he shouts. "Shells are exploding right near us! May the Lord protect us!"

One of the ladies who was singing earlier says, "We have reached the end of days." Her black dress hangs crookedly on her lean frame and she grips the top of a pew to steady herself.

"It may be so," says Mrs. Walker, who rushes among the pews, nudging anyone still resting to get up and follow the reverend. "But you must have faith. We must trust in the Lord's plans for us."

"What kind of plan is this?" says the woman in the black dress.

"Be repentant and humble before the Lord and you will be saved," says Mrs. Walker.

"I do hope so," says the woman.

Reverend Walker pushes open the massive wooden front door of the church with a loud creak. Smoke roils in. Everyone in the church files out, stumbling along behind the billowing black robe of the reverend. Frightened and disoriented, Amanda tries her hardest not to trip over her feet. The street is littered with objects that have fallen off carts—a scarf, the lid to a cooking pot, a bureau drawer. A pink ribbon, likely from someone's church bonnet, lies in a dusty curlicue.

Where there should be buildings along the slope from Main Street to the river, there are sparks and smoldering timbers. In the distance, flaming warships drift in the river, their ammunition exploding occasionally with a boom and streaks of light. Mayo's Bridge and the Danville Railroad Bridge burn, too, the water reflecting and doubling the menacing effect of the lines of flame.

Amanda is swept along in the group following Reverend Walker. Behind them, there's a tremendous crash. The roof of the church tumbles in, then catches flame. They left just in time. She begins running uphill to the grounds of Capitol Square. When she arrives, hundreds of other refugees sprawl in the grass around her. She loses sight of Reverend Walker but finds an empty spot and sits with a thud. The wind brings a bitter scent. Ashes stick to her skin. When she tries to brush off her arm, the ashes smear.

A cacophony of murmuring voices, crying children, and anguished shrillness engulfs Amanda, but she is too numb to react. She sits, blinking as people of all types make their way around her, carrying pots, pans, blankets, boots—anything they could grab from the homes they fled. When Amanda closes her eyes and tries to rest, her eyelids prickle, so she gives up. She looks east, up towards her home on Church Hill. It seems dark and calm in that direction.

"Did you hear?" a man with a soot-blackened face says as he

tries to make his way through. "Our largest warehouses are destroyed. All burned. The Yankees won't get our tobacco, but now there's nothing left. Nothing at all."

The news jolts Amanda into alertness.

"Everything on Cary near 14th?" she asks.

"I reckon so."

"That's where...that's where...my husband has his business."

"Nothing there now except a pile of ashes, I'm sorry to say."

"Were our soldiers fighting the fire?"

"Nothing much anyone could do by the time I saw it."

Amanda lies back down and puts an arm over her eyes. Out there somewhere, Edwin must be moving among the flames. Perhaps he knows about the damage to his business; perhaps he hasn't yet heard. He must be exhausted by now, stumbling, his injured eye throbbing. Worry bubbles up in her as strongly as it did in the first weeks after he enlisted. Yet she remembers the fervor that billowed through his wheat-colored eyes the night that Virginia voted to secede. His heart has always been with the Confederacy, even though Amanda now believes that he loves her, too.

When at last the sun rises, red as a welt, over the eastern hills of the city, it brings the destruction into full relief. A vast swath of blackened walls and broken chimneys lines the hill from below the capitol to the river. Smoke blankets everything, but it does not muffle the hiss and crackle of fires that continue to burn, nor the hubbub of voices around her.

In the crowd, Amanda feels completely alone. Everyone she cares about is gone, starting with her parents. Where is Edwin in this pall of gray air? Anywhere he goes, destruction must be shrouding him.

An elderly woman in a battered straw hat stands and points south towards the river. There's a line of men dressed in blue, their rifles poking up through the smoke. On horseback, they ride up the hill towards the capitol. Closer they come until Amanda can hear the rhythmic thud of hooves and see the men's pale, curious faces. Exhaustion trumps her fear that these soldiers will menace the crowd of ragged civilians. They ride right past, scattering people out of the way. A band of Negroes and assorted sympathizers follows, many shouting halleluiah. The capitol building's white columns rise in front of them like avenging angels.

A group halts, dismounts, and pulls down the Confederate flag. A chevron-shaped Massachusetts cavalry guidon rises in its place. A few people cheer, but most watch in silence.

In front of the capitol, Amanda hears more cheering and the opening lines of the "Star Spangled Banner." Someone has hoisted an American flag over the building. Its red and white stripes remind her of all the wounds she cleaned and bandaged at Mrs. Walker's hospital. She imagines leading Edwin, taking Nell and Jacob by the hand, and floating away from the ruined city, the four of them a constellation of stars in the calm square of blue.

Epilogue

Cassie

As Cassie and Julia walk off the docks along the Kanawha Canal in Richmond, stone foundations where warehouses once stood gape like rows of broken teeth. Part of the wall of a flour mill remains intact, but the windows are blown out and the rest of the building has fallen away. Charred bricks and broken glass litter swaths of the landscape. Soldiers returning home after the Confederate army's surrender at Appomattox look like ragamuffins, their hand-sewn uniforms in mismatched shades of gray. At the bottom of the hill, the canal flows serenely, as if the war hadn't ravaged the city next to it.

Though the day started out with sun, a gray sky clamps down on the warm, early May afternoon. Cassie shifts Jacob from one hip to the other, then picks her way carefully through the rubble in the rag-stuffed shoes that Missus Carter gave her for the trip to North Carolina. With familiar landmarks gone, Cassie has to pause several times to figure out where to find the Carter home.

After the Union soldiers told all the colored people in their contraband camp in North Carolina that the war had ended and they were free from slavery—and free to leave—Cassie cashed in the gold piece hidden in her hem. She bought passage to Richmond for herself, Julia, Katie, and Jacob.

"Richmond mighty broken up," says Cassie, pausing to wipe her brow with the sleeve of the dress she made from a discarded flour sack.

Julia's head swivels as she looks around, wide-eyed. "Worse than North Carolina," she says.

"It don't look like it used to here," says Cassie. "Everything gone. Trees, too."

When they reach the top of the hill at 14th Street, Cassie

sees a hand-lettered sign on a broken wooden board.

"Gin-ger-brrrrr...Gingerbread!" she reads aloud. At the contraband camp, she continued her reading lessons with a Union Army cook who came from Massachusetts. Many of the former slaves in the camp, including Julia, gathered around him during the last hour of daylight. He drew letters in the dirt with a stick and taught them how to sound out each one and fit them together into words. Cassie learned enough to be able to read a few verses of Genesis each morning.

A thick-waisted colored woman stands next to the sign.

"Mo-lasses ginger-bread," she calls out when they approach. "One penny, one square."

"No need of gingerbread, thank you," says Cassie.

Julia sets Katie down for a minute. The child stands on wobbly legs and holds her mother's skirt.

"Where you from?"

Julia and Cassie exchange a glance.

"Nowhere right now," says Cassie. "But we got some business to take care of in Richmond."

Amanda

Amanda pulls a stick through the dirt in her garden, creating a furrow about six inches deep.

"Here," she calls to her helper, a ten-year-old boy who lives down Franklin Street. He knocked on her door two weeks ago, solemn-faced and scared, asking if she had any work so he could help his family get something to eat. Amanda told him she would pay in vegetables.

Now she points out three-foot intervals where the cucumber seedlings should be planted. "Let's mark each spot with a stone and then put in a plant next to it," she says.

Nothing in the pollen-laced sunlight of this early May afternoon in the garden suggests that Richmond so recently burned and that General Robert E. Lee surrendered at Appomattox a week later. In quick succession, the Confederate legislature dissolved and President Lincoln was assassinated. The fire in Richmond spared the Carter home on its perch high above the city. Its windows didn't even break in the concussion of exploding shells.

It took two days for a messenger to bring the letter to Amanda with the news about Edwin.

> *Mrs. Carter,*
> *As an officer in the Second Battalion of Richmond Reserves, I have the regretful task of informing you of the death of your husband, Lt. Col. Edwin Carter. On 2 April he joined our reserves and immediately carried out orders to fire Mayo's Bridge and march toward Burkeville Jct. On 6 April the artillery opened on us, fatally wounding Lt. Col. Carter. He fought bravely to the end. His body was buried near Sayler's Creek.*
> *Yours,*
> *Capt. Wm Simon*

After Amanda received the letter, she put on Edwin's dressing gown and sat all night in his armchair, cradling his unlit pipe in her hand. In the morning, she went out back and circled the half-cultivated garden, promising to plant a linden sapling in his honor alongside Nell's camellia. She still sleeps in his dressing gown—if she can sleep at all. The house echoes around her like a broken promise.

When the back gate creaks open, Amanda looks up and sees a small, dark-skinned woman wearing a red headscarf making her way up the path with a baby in her arms. A willowy, light-skinned woman follows her with a girl on her hip.

"Cassie!" Amanda shouts, running to her.

Cassie stops walking and Amanda practically collides with her.

"Jacob, Jacob, Jacob," Amanda intones, taking the baby from Cassie, holding him to her breast and rocking him. His blanket falls to the ground. She nuzzles him, ignoring his sour smell from four days of travel. He already looks different from when he left, his face rounder and pinker than she remembers it. She touches his right palm and he grasps her finger.

Finally, she looks up and says, "Mrs. Spencer wrote to me and said you never came. I didn't know...I thought you never...Oh, Cassie! Whatever happened to you?"

The boy who is helping Amanda comes back from the end of the row. "I've laid out all the stones," he says, gaping at the group.

"You may take your leave now," she says. "Thank you."

He stares before nodding and scurrying out the back gate.

Cassie surveys the half-planted garden, her gaze sweeping from the back wall to the back porch.

"Miss Nell? Where Miss Nell at?" Cassie asks.

Amanda's face twists. "Oh, Cassie."

"Bad news, from the look of it."

"She was hit by a carriage right after you left. I was careless and I let her run ahead of me. She thought she saw you and..."

Cassie walks to the back porch step and sinks down, face in her hands. She puts the satchel on the ground by her feet.

"It's all my fault," chokes out Amanda. "I never should have let her run ahead of me. But you know how headstrong she was."

"Lord have mercy," says Cassie. "She gone to Glory Land."

Amanda begins crying and sits on the step, too, balancing Jacob on her knee. "If only I hadn't sent you away...," she begins.

"Missus, easy, now. Miss Nell be walking with the Lord," says Cassie, looking across so she meets Amanda's eyes. "Must have been her time, even though it seem too soon."

Amanda pulls out a handkerchief with one hand and wipes her eyes. "And then Edwin, I mean Master Carter..."

"He gone to Glory too?"

"Everyone is gone," Amanda says, clinging tightly to Jacob.

Cassie is silent a long moment, rubbing the toe of her shoe in the dirt. She looks up and says, "Sometimes, the Lord work in mysterious ways."

Amanda looks across the garden at Julia, who stands behind Katie, holding the girl's hands as Katie puts one wobbly foot forward, then the other. "Who is this with you?"

"My daughter and my grandbaby."

"What? How on earth?"

"Missus, that a long story. Can we trouble you for some water and something to eat?"

"Of course, of course. Come in," says Amanda, leading the way up the back porch.

"How your cooking coming along?"

"Well, I have a lot to learn," says Amanda and laughs.

Cassie laughs, too, and shakes her head.

Amanda sets Jacob on a pillow in the corner of the kitchen, where he falls asleep, each of his tiny snores keeping glorious rhythm to her steps into the pantry. Cassie and Julia help her make rice and boiled sweet potatoes flavored with chopped sage from the garden. When the food is ready, Amanda pulls a dining room chair up to the kitchen table and says, "I'll eat with you tonight. No need to serve me."

It's dusk by the time Cassie finishes telling about their journey south and their time in the contraband camp.

When Cassie yawns, Amanda stands and clears her throat. "I've been meaning...well, I'd like to ask...will you stay on here? There's room for all of you. It won't be like before. I'll do my share and I'll pay you wages."

Cassie shakes her head. "We ask you to stay just for tonight, Missus. We going back by our old homeplace. Far as I know, Clancy, he still there. And my son, too."

"Oh, Cassie, I never should have sent you away. It was too much to ask. I'm sure there was a suitable family for Jacob in Richmond."

Cassie makes a sweeping motion with the back of her hand.

"Missus, that be the Lord working in mysterious ways," she says.

"What's the mystery in heartbreak?" says Amanda, twisting her napkin.

Julia stands and begins clearing the dishes.

"You aim to keep Jacob here?" asks Cassie.

"Edwin's brother asked me to move out there to live with him and his wife. I was going to get through the gardening season and go in November. But I won't be able to do that anymore. Not with Jacob."

"You want to go? Then go. Tell them you keeping a war orphan. Plenty of those around."

Amanda stands to help Julia with the dishes and says, "No more lies. I'll stay right here as a war widow with a baby."

From the pillow, Jacob begins to cry. Amanda picks him up and brings him back into the kitchen.

"What does he eat these days?" Amanda asks.

Julia begins to unbutton her dress.

"Oh, my goodness. You kept him alive all this time," Amanda says. "I never...well, I never...well, thank you!"

Julia nods calmly while Amanda splutters.

Amanda turns to Cassie and says, "Come outside and see where I'm going to plant a new camellia bush for Nell."

They step onto the back porch. Humid air softens the edges on the just-opening blossoms of the magnolia tree. Their heavy, sweet scent drifts past. Beyond that, Amanda can hear the faint tumble of water over rocks in the James River.

"You and Jacob, you going to do just fine," says Cassie.

"Thank you, Cassie. Oh, I wish you'd stay."

"Time for me to do for my own self now. And my family."

Julia walks out with Jacob in her arms. "And now it's time for me to do for mine," says Amanda, reaching for Jacob, then leading the way down to the garden.

ACKNOWLEDGMENTS

Any novel is a labor of love, and a historical novel is also a labor of research. To better understand and recreate Richmond during the Civil War years, I read and reread many books by historians. Especially helpful were *Ashes of Glory: Richmond at War* by Ernest B. Furgurson (New York: Vintage Books, 1996) and *Richmond Burning: The Last Days of the Confederate Capital* by Nelson Lankford (New York: Viking, 2002). The digitized letters from the Virginia Military Institute Archives and in the Valley of the Shadow Project, part of the Virginia Center for Digital History at the University of Virginia, revealed a range of voices of Civil War soldiers and their loved ones. Collections of slave narratives, especially *We Lived in a Little Cabin in the Yard*, edited by Belinda Hurmence (Winston-Salem: John F. Blair, 1994), helped me imagine Cassie's life. To recreate daily life in Richmond, I read the *Richmond Daily Dispatch* newspaper as well as Mary Boykin Chesnut's *A Diary from Dixie* and primary sources compiled in *A Richmond Reader*, edited by Maurice Duke and Daniel P. Jordan (Chapel Hill: University of North Carolina Press, 1983). For recipes, I went to *The Confederate Receipt Book*, originally published in Richmond in 1863. I also used maps, articles, and other material about Civil War Richmond posted on the mdgorman.com website.

After the novel took shape, for seeing it through publication, I thank Director Marc A. Jolley and the team at Mercer University Press. I also thank Kathie Bennett of Magic Time Literary Agency for connecting me with Mercer.

Writers who read and commented on early drafts—Pat Carr, Mary Sullivan, and Lynne Griffin—each helped me hone the manuscript. The late historian and author Jim Green also encouraged and guided me. Members of my reading group—Kay Cahill Allison, Jody Feinberg, Judy Gelman, Laurie Hutcheson, and Susan Katcher—provided insightful comments. My work also benefited from the literary community at the Chautauqua Writers' Center, where I received wise advice about publishing fiction, especially from Laura Kasischke. In the Boston area, I thank the community at GrubStreet Inc. and its artistic director, Christopher Castellani, as well as Barbara Helfgott Hyett and the members of her Workshop for Publishing Poets. For legal advice, I thank Joel Shames.

For believing in my project from its inception—and putting up with my endless forays into the nineteenth century—I thank my family: my son, Jordan, my first reader; my daughter, Martha, for helping me understand Nell's character; and my husband, George who patiently read draft after draft, challenging and encouraging me along the way. My mother, Ann, shared with me her collection of Virginia history books and tried her best to answer my endless questions about the "olden days." Finally, I thank my sister, Janet, who had faith that I would one day publish the book she read in its early stages but who passed away before she could see it.

ABOUT THE AUTHOR

Clara Silverstein, raised in Richmond, Virginia, is a historian and the author of the memoir *White Girl: A Story of School Desegregation*, and three cookbooks. Her articles and essays have appeared on NPR's "All Things Considered" and in the *Oxford Encyclopedia of Food and Drink in America*, *American Heritage*, *Runner's World*, and *The Boston Globe*. The former program director of the Chautauqua Writers' Center, she has taught at GrubStreet and Boston University. She lives in the Boston area.